SWEET VALLEY HIGH

HARD CHOICES

Written by
Kate William

Created by
FRANCINE PASCAL

BANTAM BOOKS

NEW YORK · TORONTO · LONDON · SYDNEY · AUCKLAND

RL6, IL age 12 and up

HARD CHOICES
A Bantam Book / February 1988

Sweet Valley High is a registered trademark of Francine Pascal

Conceived by Francine Pascal

Produced by Daniel Weiss Associates, Inc.
27 West 20th Street
New York, NY 10011

Cover art by James Mathewuse

ISBN 0-553-27006-0

Published simultaneously in the United States and Canada

---

*Bantam Books are published by Bantam Books, a division of Bantam Doubleday
Dell Publishing Group, Inc. Its trademark, consisting of the words "Bantam
Books" and the portrayal of a rooster, is Registered in U.S. Patent and Trademark
Office and in other countries. Marca Registrada. Bantam Books, 666 Fifth Avenue,
New York, New York 10103.*

PRINTED IN THE UNITED STATES OF AMERICA

O   0 9 8 7 6 5

HARD CHOICES

"Enid?" Her grandmother's insistent voice reached her from the living room. "Enid, I need my medicine."

Choking back tears, Enid stared out the front door watching her mother leave for the evening. *This can't be happening*, she thought wildly. *My mother doesn't really expect me not to see Hugh tonight.*

Enid was trembling with anger as she walked into the living room. Her grandmother looked up from her magazine and smiled faintly, "Enid, please bring me my medicine."

Enid stared in disbelief. Her grandmother had just ruined her weekend—and she was smiling! Just then the door bell rang.

Enid went slowly to the front door. It was Hugh. Before he could speak, she said bluntly, "I can't go."

For a moment he regarded her without speaking. The bouquet of flowers he was holding fell to his side.

"My grandmother says she's sick. I can't leave her."

"I can't believe you're breaking another date," Hugh said. "Do you think this is funny or something? Is that it?"

Too tired and upset to argue, Enid leaned her forehead against the door and muttered, "Just go to the party without me, Hugh."

"Listen," Hugh said. "Give me a call sometime when you've got a few free minutes. Maybe I'll be around." He threw the flowers down on the ground, turned, and strode to his car. Enid watched, tears streaming down her cheeks.

Bantam Books in the Sweet Valley High Series
Ask your bookseller for the books you have missed

HARD CHOICES

One

"How long are you going to be at Enid's?" Jessica Wakefield tapped her fingers impatiently on the steering wheel of the red Fiat convertible and turned to her sister, who was sitting in the passenger seat. "I told Lila and Cara I'd meet them at the Dairi Burger at four-thirty," Jessica added.

Elizabeth Wakefield sent her identical twin a look of exasperation as they sat parked at a curb in a residential section of Sweet Valley. "Well, Enid and I are almost finished moving her stuff, so I guess I can be ready at quarter past, Jess."

But to be perfectly realistic, she added to herself, Jessica's definition of being on time was pretty flexible. Whenever Jessica Wakefield arrived was when things got started—at least in Jessica's opinion. And besides, she never wore a watch, so it was anybody's guess when she might turn up. So Elizabeth had learned at a young age not to rely too heavily on her twin's punctuality.

In a way, their different attitude about time was a perfect example of the differences between them. Elizabeth was only four minutes older than Jessica, but it was a standing joke in their family that Elizabeth had been born on time—and Jessica four minutes late! That had been more or less the pattern for all their sixteen years.

Even though at first glance Elizabeth and Jessica seemed to be absolutely identical—from their slim size-six figures and blond hair to their striking blue-green eyes and the dimple in each girl's left cheek—they were as different on the inside as two people could be. Jessica dashed through life like a bolt of lightning, but Elizabeth thought things through before getting involved, often sorting out her ideas by writing in her journal. But in spite of their wildly different styles, the Wakefield twins shared a special bond that no one else could understand.

Jessica sent her sister a twinkling smile. "Then I'll see you at a quarter past four, Liz. On the dot."

"OK, Jess," Elizabeth agreed as she opened

the door and stepped out of the Fiat. She held back a grin as she repeated, "On the dot."

With a carefree wave, Jessica put the car in gear and roared away from the curb. Elizabeth chuckled to herself and headed up to the walk to her best friend's house.

"Where do you want me to put these, Enid?" Elizabeth asked, carrying an armload of books and staggering through the door of the attic bedroom.

Enid Rollins turned around, "Uh, just on the floor in the corner, I guess, Liz," she said absently. "I'll have to figure out something for bookshelves pretty soon."

"Whew, what a load!" Elizabeth gasped as she put the the books down. She leaned against the wall and slid to the floor. Pushing her bangs off her forehead, she looked around her critically. "This could be a really nice room, Enid, you know?"

Enid nodded eagerly. "I know. Mom and I decided all it needs are a few touches to make it really homey. We saw a pretty rug downtown that would look great up here. And I thought some plants would look nice too, but for now . . ."

For now, they couldn't really afford those extra touches, Enid thought to herself. As a single parent, Mrs. Rollins couldn't make her salary stretch to redecorate *two* rooms in the house at the same time; and at the moment they were working hard to make Enid's old bedroom a new home for Mrs. Langevin, Enid's grandmother, who was coming to live with them.

With a happy sigh, Enid dropped down on the floor beside Elizabeth and crossed her legs in front of her. "I can't wait till Nana gets here, Liz. You'll love her as much as I do, I know it. She's so funny and sweet and—and grandmotherly!" She laughed. "And when she starts baking cookies—look out!"

"Whoa! Sounds serious." Elizabeth smiled. "I'm so happy for you, Enid. Really."

"Thanks, Liz. Me, too." Even since her grandmother had decided to move in with them, Enid had been very excited. Some of her happiest childhood memories were of Nana—and Gramps, too, when he was still alive, but it was her grandmother's loving green eyes and snow-white curls that always sprang to mind whenever Enid thought about those magical visits to the rambling old house in Chicago.

But when Mr. Langevin had died a few months earlier, it didn't make much sense for his widow to live alone in that big house. So even though the Rollinses' house was much smaller, there had never been any question about finding room for Nana. Enid didn't like having

4

to give up her pretty bedroom and move up to the attic, but her grandmother was worth it. They certainly couldn't ask *her* to climb those extra stairs! Enid was willing to make any sacrifice for her grandmother's sake.

There were footsteps on the attic stairs, and Mrs. Rollins, who had taken the afternoon off from her job, appeared in the doorway with a pile of linens in her arms. "What's this? Sitting down on the job, girls?" she joked. "Elizabeth Wakefield, you're a terrible influence on my daughter."

"That's right," Enid chimed in, trying to suppress a laugh. "It's all her fault, Mom."

"Hey, no fair ganging up on me!" Elizabeth protested. But she had been around the Rollinses enough to know that they were only teasing.

Enid scrambled to her feet and held out a hand to help Elizabeth up. "Here. Help me make this bed, will you?" she asked, shaking out a fitted sheet. "And stop causing trouble," she added, the smile on her face betraying the joke.

"The abuse I take," Elizabeth muttered in an injured tone. "Every time I come over here, it's nothing but nag, nag, nag."

When they finished making the bed, Mrs. Rollins reappeared in the doorway with an armload of Enid's clothes.

"Sorry, honey. I know there really isn't any-

5

where for you to put your clothes in here yet, but the closet in Nana's room is so small—and I'm not sure how many things she'll be bringing."

A look of dismay crossed Enid's face as she took the dresses and skirts. "What am I going to do with this stuff?" She glanced quickly around the room.

"Maybe we could put some nails in the wall," Elizabeth suggested. "Then you could hang up a cord to put the hangers on."

"Hmmm." Pursing her lips, Mrs. Rollins regarded the unfinished attic walls and shrugged. "I guess that's what we'll have to do for now. Later on we can get some kind of wardrobe, honey."

Enid nodded and tossed the bundle of clothes on the bed. "Oh, well—it's not such a big deal." She met Elizabeth's gaze briefly, then looked away.

At that moment, a furious honking reached their ears from the street. Enid and Elizabeth crossed to one of the attic windows and looked out.

"Wouldn't you know it?" Elizabeth said with a laugh. "For once in her life, Jess is on time. I hate to leave you stranded," she continued, glancing around at the mess. "Hey, why don't you come with us?"

"Oh—well, I—" Enid frowned.

Her mother put a hand on her shoulder. "Go on, honey, you can always finish later."

The horn sounded again, and Elizabeth picked up her jacket. "I'll try to keep her calm until you get ready."

Enid nodded. "Thanks. I'll be down in a second."

As Elizabeth ran quickly down the stairs, Mrs. Rollins put both hands on Enid's shoulders and looked intently into her face.

"Sweetheart, I want you to know how proud I am of you for being so generous and helpful about moving and getting ready for Nana."

Enid blushed. "It's OK, Mom. You know I'd do anything for her."

"Of course you would, but I want to make sure you realize what it means."

"What it means?" Enid repeated as her mother led her to the bed and sat her down.

"Nana is going to have a very difficult time adjusting to life here, and we're going to have to try very hard to make it as easy for her as possible," Mrs. Rollins said. She took Enid's hands in her own and smiled tenderly. "When Gramps died, a big part of her life ended, too. Just remember that, will you?"

"Sure, Mom. I understand. Really."

"I know you do, sweetie." Mrs. Rollins drew Enid close in a tight hug. "Oooooh. I love you so much. You know that?"

7

Enid smiled and squeezed back. "I know. Me, too." She wished they could stay that way forever—her and her mother, and now her grandmother, too. She felt a momentary sting of jealousy as she thought of her mother's boyfriend, Richard Cernak, and the time her mother spent with him. If it weren't for his taking so much of her mother's attention, things would be perfect.

"Now get out of here—your friends are waiting for you." With a playful shove, Mrs. Rollins pushed Enid out of the room. Enid grabbed her canvas shoulder bag in the downstairs hall and ran outside to join the Wakefield twins.

The Fiat glided into the parking lot of the Dairi Burger, and Jessica maneuvered it deftly into a space. The three girls made their way across the parking lot, which was packed with cars—typical for a Friday afternoon. At the door Jessica went her own way, spotting her two best friends, Lila Fowler and Cara Walker, sitting in a booth. Elizabeth and Enid found an empty table across the room and sat down gratefully.

"You stay here," Enid suggested, instantly rising to her feet, "and I'll go get us some sodas. It's so crowded today we'd probably lose the table if we both went."

Elizabeth grinned up at her friend. "OK—make it my usual, bartender."

"One root beer, coming up!" With a salute, Enid turned and picked her way across the popular after-school hangout.

"Liz! Hi, I can't believe I found you."

Looking up in surprise, Elizabeth saw Penny Ayala, the editor-in-chief of Sweet Valley High's student newspaper, *The Oracle*, hurrying toward her.

"What's up, Pen? You look like you're in a panic."

Rolling her eyes, Penny sank down into Enid's empty seat and dumped a manila folder on the table. "That is not the word for it, Liz. Listen, we had a major problem with the typesetter this week, and I just got the proofs for the next edition *today*. Can you do me a huge favor and proofread some of them this afternoon or tonight?"

"Sure, no problem," Elizabeth said quickly, pulling the pages toward her. Writing the school's "Eyes and Ears" gossip column was only part of the work she did on the paper. She also wrote articles and, like everyone else on the staff, helped out with editorial duties such as proofreading.

As Penny left wearing a grateful smile, Elizabeth ran her eyes down the first page. Instantly she spotted a headline that caught her atten-

9

tion: "Filmmaker Announces Showcase for Student Documentaries." Her curiosity was piqued, and Elizabeth read the short piece quickly. Jackson Croft, a famous film producer and director, was the father of one of Elizabeth's classmates, Susan Stewart.

"What are you reading?"

Elizabeth looked up as Enid rejoined her with two sodas. "Listen to this, Enid," she said as she reached for her root beer. "Susan's father is sponsoring a showcase for student documentaries. Anyone who's interested can have a one-hour video shown. I wonder if anyone from our school will make one."

"Why don't you?"

Elizabeth met Enid's gaze across the table and shrugged. "I don't know. I guess I never really thought about doing anything like that," she said. "Besides, I wouldn't have any idea what to make a documentary about."

Enid rolled her eyes. "Yeah, you're always such a creative desert."

"Oh, shut up!" Elizabeth regarded her best friend and smiled, "Well, maybe I'll think about it."

"You could do a documentary about grandmothers moving in with their kids' families," Enid quipped, her eyes twinkling above the rim of her paper cup.

"Hmm. Know anyone like that I might be able to interview?"

Enid shrugged nonchalantly. "I could probably think of *one* person."

Giggling, Elizabeth looked around the familiar interior of the Dairi Burger. It was packed with students from Sweet Valley High, and her own junior class was well represented. In a booth by the window, her twin was deep in conversation with Lila and Cara. Next to them, six members of the soccer team were squeezed in around John Pfeiffer, sports editor of *The Oracle*. Sally and Dana Larson, cousins, were just sitting down at a nearby table with plates of burgers and fries.

Everywhere Elizabeth looked, she saw friends and familiar faces, and a warm glow of pride and happiness washed over her. It always struck her as special that although Sweet Valley was a bustling town, it somehow managed to feel small and friendly at the same time. She loved her hometown. Smiling fondly, she rested her chin in her hands and gazed off into space.

"I know that look," Enid said, leaning back and folding her arms across her chest.

"Oh, yeah? What look is that?"

"The Elizabeth-Wakefield-creative-inspiration look," her friend replied with a smile.

Elizabeth snorted. "If you only knew how *un*-creative I was being. I was just feeling senti-

11

mental about living in the most wonderful town in the whole world, that's all."

"Oh, that's all!"

At that moment Jessica rushed over to the table. "Ready to go, Liz?"

"Oh—" Elizabeth looked questioningly at her best friend.

"I can get a ride from the Larsons," Enid assured her. "I'll talk to you later."

With a grateful smile, Elizabeth stood up, and gathered the proofs together. She would finish them at home that night and drop them off the next morning at Penny's. "OK. Oh, and, Enid—good luck tomorrow when your grandmother gets here. I can't wait to meet her."

Enid's eyes shone, and she nodded happily. "Thanks. I can't wait either."

Two

Enid slammed the front door behind her and took the stairs two at a time. A rapid glance at her watch told her it was one-fifteen: her mother and grandmother would be back from the airport at any minute. She had stayed behind in order to make some last-minute preparations.

Hurrying into the bathroom, she set down the packages she was carrying, then unwrapped one of them. The scent of lavender immediately filled the room as she opened the box of pretty, heart-shaped soaps she had bought at the Valley Mall that morning. She arranged them in a dainty porcelain dish by the sink.

"Nana will like that," she said aloud, brimming with satisfaction and pride. The soaps had been expensive, but her grandmother was worth it.

Next she picked up a tissue-wrapped bouquet of flowers—freesias, carnations, baby's breath, and three white rosebuds. Holding them up to her face, she breathed deeply, inhaling the heady fragrance. Then she arranged them carefully in a vase and took it into her old bedroom. Between the soaps and the flowers, she had just about exhausted her allowance. But the look on her grandmother's face when she saw them would be more than ample compensation.

"There," she said, setting the vase on the bureau and looking around appraisingly. Her old room had been transformed: new curtains billowed out from the open windows, a new bedspread and new pillow shams decorated the bed, and family photographs had been arranged on the bedside table. Enid could just imagine her grandmother's pleased smile.

With a contented sigh, Enid sank down on the bed. It was going to be so wonderful to have her grandmother there. She loved sitting and talking to her grandmother. And, of course, Nana would be home all the time, not like Mrs. Rollins, who spent so much time working. Enid and her grandmother could talk and play Scrabble and go to the movies together, anytime.

Enid studied the room one last time. It was a pretty room, and she realized that she would miss it. But she also knew she didn't regret having to move.

Tapping her foot impatiently, Enid checked her watch again. *There must be a delay at the airport*, she told herself.

For a moment she considered taking some time to call her boyfriend, Hugh Grayson. Lately they had been having some problems with their relationship that she wanted to clear up.

Since he went to nearby Big Mesa High School and didn't live in Sweet Valley, they couldn't see each other every day. At first, it hadn't made any difference. When they had met a few months earlier, there was an instant spark of attraction, and they had both gone out of their way to make time for each other.

But recently it had been getting harder and harder to do. They each had their separate school activities and different circles of friends. Enid shook her head; she and Hugh definitely needed to spend some time together. But for the moment . . .

A car door slammed outside, and Enid ran to the window. Her mother's car had just pulled up to the curb. She could just make out the white-haired figure in the front passenger seat.

"Nana!" Enid rushed out of the room and raced downstairs and outside. As she ran to the car, Enid caught a fleeting look from her mother. But it didn't register. She opened the door and leaned in to hug her grandmother. "Oh, Nana! I can't believe you're here."

"Enid, hello, dear." Mrs. Langevin's voice sounded faint and slightly strained.

Enid pulled back and got her first real look at her grandmother. The green eyes looking back at her had lost their bright sparkle, and the woman seemed much older and frailer then Enid remembered. Enid tried to hide her surprise. "Here. Let me help you out, Nana."

"Thank you, dear." Laying a thin hand on Enid's arm, Mrs. Langevin swung her legs out of the car with difficulty and slowly rose to her feet. Enid felt the hand grip her wrist with an almost desperate hold, and she glanced quickly to the back of the car where her mother was opening the trunk. They exchanged an apprehensive look. Nana seemed so weak and worn out. Where was the vital, energetic grandmother she remembered?

Mrs. Langevin looked toward the house and set her mouth in a grim line. "So many steps to the front door," she murmured faintly.

"Oh, I'll help you, don't worry about that," Enid said quickly. She put a hand under her grandmother's elbow, and together they walked slowly up to the door. Mrs. Rollins followed with two suitcases.

"Thank you, dear. You're so good to me," Mrs. Langevin said to Enid. "What would I do without you?"

Enid felt a warm flush wash over her cheeks.

But whether it was love or embarrassment, she didn't know. It was confusing to find her grandmother so different from the way she remembered her. "Don't be silly," she said lightly, opening the door and helping her grandmother inside. "You're here now, so there's nothing to worry about. Let me show you your room," she continued quickly.

Her grandmother clutched her bulky, old-fashioned purse tightly against her chest and looked around. She sighed heavily. "Do we have to go upstairs?"

"Well—yes, Nana. Just hold on to the banister, and there's a landing halfway up."

"Thank you, dear. I'm just so tired after my trip. I hate to be a bother."

"You're not a bother, Nana. Really," Enid insisted. Her heart lurched painfully, and she looked over her shoulder again at her mother. Mrs. Rollins smiled and nodded encouragement.

"I'll bring your suitcases up, Mother. I know you'll be anxious to settle in."

When they reached the top of the stairs, Mrs. Langevin stepped into her new room. Enid found herself smiling with anticipation.

There was a pause as Mrs. Langevin surveyed the room. "It's . . . so much smaller than I remembered," she said finally, in a worried tone. "Where am I going to put all my things? I brought most of my little treasures with me, and now—"

17

"Well, we can put your things anywhere you like, Mother," Mrs. Rollins assured her briskly. "If they're all over the house, it will make you feel even more at home." She set the luggage at the end of the bed. "And if you need more closet space—"

"Don't bother about me," Mrs. Langevin said as she lowered herself carefully onto the bed. "I don't want to put anyone to any trouble."

Mrs. Rollins opened her mouth as though she were going to speak, but closed it and met Enid's troubled gaze.

Puzzled, Enid raised her eyebrows, then turned back to grandmother. "Nana, how about if I help you unpack? You can sit there on the bed and tell me where you want me to put your things, OK?"

Mrs. Langevin closed her eyes wearily. "I think I'd just like to rest for a while, Enid, dear. I'm so tired after the trip. It was exhausting getting to the airport . . . and the plane was delayed. . . ." Her voice trailed off, and she shook her head absently.

Enid nodded quickly. "Of course, Nana. I'll help you later. We'll leave you alone and let you take a nap."

"Thank you, dear. Oh, and, Adele—these flowers . . ."

"Yes, Mother?"

Enid held her breath.

18

"I'm afraid they might have pollen. I don't think I should have them in my room."

"Well, I'll just take them away, Mother. There's no problem," Mrs. Rollins said soothingly. "We don't want you to get hay fever." She crossed quickly to the bureau for the flowers and sent Enid an apologetic smile.

With a last, anxious glance at the frail woman on the bed, Enid followed her mother out the door and down the stairs. Silently they walked into the living room and sat down. Enid didn't trust herself to speak. It was more than disappointment about her grandmother's reaction to the flowers. Something was very wrong.

"Enid?"

Her mother was smiling sadly at her. With a slight catch in her voice, Enid asked, "Mom, what's happened to her?"

"Oh, honey." Mrs. Rollins leaned back in her chair and rubbed her eyes. "I guess she suddenly decided she's an old woman. Moving out of the old house probably brought it all home to her. I'm hoping she'll spring back pretty soon. But in the meantime we'll just have to make an extra effort."

For a moment Enid was afraid she might cry. It seemed so unfair that her grandmother had to be uprooted like that. Obviously, it had taken its toll.

Echoing Enid's thoughts, Mrs. Rollins said

softly, "She seems much more dependent than I expected her to be." She wrinkled her nose. "I wonder if I should tell Richard not to come over for dinner tonight."

"I don't know, Mom," Enid stared at the floor.

"I mean, I thought it would be a good idea if she met new people right away—and Richard is so eager to meet her."

All Enid could think of was her grandmother's frail, careworn face. She had never really thought of her grandmother as being old before. But there was no question about it. She was an old woman.

"It must be just the traveling," she said slowly.

Mrs. Rollins nodded. "You're probably right. I'll just ask Richard not to stay too long this evening. I don't want to push Mother on her first night."

A heavy silence descended, and Enid glanced across at her mother, trying to put her jumbled worries into words. Ever since her parents' divorce, she and her mother had been very close, friends as well as mother and daughter. Yet Enid couldn't bring herself to say out loud the things she was thinking, even to her mother.

An hour later, Enid was staring morosely out the living room window, while her mother was in the kitchen.

"Yoo-hoo! Anybody home?" a voice cooed from the top of the stairs.

Enid jumped to her feet and headed toward the stairs. "Nana!" Mrs. Rollins walked from the kitchen into the hallway. They both stopped at the foot of the steps.

"I feel so much better," Mrs. Langevin said as she felt her way downstairs carefully, one hand clutching the rail. "Help an old lady?" she teased, smiling at Enid.

"Sure, Nana," Enid ran up the steps and held out her arm. The relief at seeing her grandmother recovered was almost overpowering.

"Now just help me get into the living room, and I'll sit there for a while," Nana said. "That's fine."

Enid and her mother rushed around, pulling up a footstool, plumping up pillows, and making Mrs. Langevin as comfortable as possible. The elderly woman smiled and held up a hand in protest. "Now, now—don't fuss over me. I don't want to be a bother."

"You're not a bother, Nana. We're just so happy to see you feeling better." Enid perched on the arm of the couch, ready to spring at a moment's notice.

Mrs. Rollins sat next to Enid. "That's right, Mother. We're so glad you're here. Really."

"And Mom has been all over town finding out things you can do," Enid rushed on excit-

21

edly. "There's a senior center that has classes and programs—"

"And the library has a large-print book exchange with other libraries around the state," Mrs. Rollins broke in. "You'll be able to get almost any book you want."

Smiling faintly, Mrs. Langevin shook her head. "No, no, Adele, dear. I don't want to be a burden to you. I'm not going to make you drive me all over town."

"But, Mother, you still have your driver's license, don't you?"

Mrs. Langevin pressed her lips together firmly. "Dear, I'm not sure I feel up to driving in a strange town right away."

"Besides," Enid put in quickly, "I'd be happy to show you around, Nana. It's no bother at all, really."

"You're so sweet. Enid. But I don't want to put you to any trouble."

"Nana—"

"Mother," Mrs. Rollins said patiently. She reached for Enid's hand and squeezed briefly before letting go. "Why don't I just pick up a bulletin from the senior center, and if there's anything going on that you think you might like to do, we'll arrange for you to be there. How would that be? There's no hurry."

Mrs. Langevin sighed. "All right, dear."

The atmosphere grew slightly uncomfortable,

and Enid jumped up nervously. "Mom, why don't you go do that grocery shopping—and—and Nana and I can stay here and tell secrets." She forced a laugh.

"Good idea." Mrs. Rollins was suddenly brisk and businesslike. "Mother, is there anything special you'd like me to pick up for you?"

"Thank you, Adele. But I don't want to—"

"*Mother!*" Exasperated, Mrs. Rollins spoke more sharply than she had intended. She took a deep breath and smiled. "I'm perfectly happy to get anything you'd like to make you feel comfortable. Some fresh fruit—or a special tea? Anything?"

Her mother shook her head. "No, thank you."

For a moment Mrs. Rollins stood still in the center of the room. Then she shrugged and went out into the hall, leaving Enid and her grandmother alone in the living room.

"So." Enid patted the arms of the chair she had moved to. "How about a cup of tea, Nana?"

"Were you planning to have some yourself, Enid?"

"Yes," Enid lied glibly, meeting her grandmother's eyes. She didn't want her grandmother to refuse just out of courtesy. "So I'll make enough for two."

Mrs. Langevin held out her hand, and Enid rushed over to take it. Her grandmother gave her a grateful smile. "You're so good to me, dear. So good."

"That's OK, Nana," Enid said, made slightly uncomfortable again by the change in her grandmother's attitude. She had always been so bustling and independent. "You just wait right here, and I'll be back in a second."

Hurrying from the room, Enid ran into her mother, who was just shrugging into her raincoat in the front hall. Their eyes locked for a moment, and then at the same time, they both looked back toward the living room.

"Just give her some time," Mrs. Rollins whispered, touching Enid's shoulder gently. "Don't forget it's a big adjustment for her."

"Yeah, Mom. See you later."

As Enid shut the door behind her mother, a feeling of uneasiness crept over her. So far, this wasn't turning out the way she had expected at all.

Her grandmother's voice broke into her thoughts. "Enid? Are you making the tea?"

"Yes, Nana. I'll be right there." Forcing herself to ignore her worries, Enid ran to the kitchen to put the kettle on.

Three

"Time to roll over, Liz. You're getting a little overcooked on that side."

With a drowsy groan, Elizabeth propped herself up on her elbow and squinted against the bright Pacific Ocean glare. "You'd think living in California all my life I wouldn't get burned anymore," she said, shading her eyes as she looked at her boyfriend, Jeffrey French. She inched up the edge of her turquoise maillot and shook her head at the bright pink line. "But I guess I still can."

Jeffrey just smiled and leaned over to tickle her toes.

"Hey, cut that out!"

"How about going in for a swim?" Jeffrey

asked with a teasing grin. "Or do I have to throw you in?"

"Don't you even think about it," Elizabeth warned. Jeffrey's face fell, and she laughed forgivingly. "Go on in. I don't feel like swimming."

Elizabeth smiled happily as she watched him stroll confidently down to the water's edge; she loved his lean, muscular look. He stood ankle-deep in the foaming surf for a moment and then dived into an oncoming wave. He swam over to where Bill Chase, a fellow junior at Sweet Valley High, was floating lazily on his surfboard. As the two started to talk, Elizabeth let her gaze wander away.

Not more than ten feet from her, her twin and Lila were planted amid a huge assortment of towels, clothes, magazines, radios, soda cans, makeup bags, and other paraphernalia they seemed to feel was vital to a day at the beach. Near the lifeguard station cheerleaders Sandra Bacon and Jean West were practicing handstands and cartwheels. Their boyfriends, Manuel Lopez and Tom McKay, watched admiringly.

An indignant scream brought Elizabeth's attention back to her twin. Water was dripping from Jessica's hair and shoulders, and Lila was doubled up and shaking with laughter. Standing behind them with a bucket in his hands was Winston Egbert, Sweet Valley High's junior class clown. "Gee, sorry, Jess. I'm such a klutz," he said apologetically. "I just tripped. Honest."

"Yeah, right, Win," Jessica retorted, wiping her face. "I really believe that."

"Gee, I don't know, Jess," Lila said, trying to sound serious. "You were just complaining about how hot it was."

Jessica shot her a withering glance, and Elizabeth lay back, closing her eyes again. It was a familiar scene—all of it. Every weekend she could count on seeing friends at the beach, relaxing, doing homework, or just having fun. That was one of the things she appreciated the most about living in Sweet Valley: it might be predictable, but she loved the warmth and cozy familiarity of it. Of course, Jessica often grew tired of what she called "the same old boring things," but that was just Jessica. As far as Elizabeth was concerned, that was part of what made Sweet Valley such a wonderful town.

Elizabeth's thoughts strayed back to the article she had read the previous day. It *would* be fun to make a documentary, but Elizabeth couldn't think of anything she felt confident enough to report on so thoroughly. If only she could . . .

She sat up suddenly, looking around with growing eagerness. Why couldn't she make a documentary about Sweet Valley? That was definitely something she was an expert on. The more she thought about it, the better the idea seemed.

Elizabeth wrapped her arms around her knees and bit her lip in concentration. "Why not?" she said aloud, smiling broadly as Jeffrey ran up.

"Why not what?" he echoed, reaching for a towel.

"What do you think about making a documentary about Sweet Valley?"

"Making a—" He broke off, a look of surprise on his face. He flung the damp towel over his shoulder as he sat down. "Do you mean *you* want to make it? Why?"

"Yes," Elizabeth said, "I want to make it." She explained about the contest. Then she shifted onto her knees and leaned forward eagerly. "And *you* could film it!" she added, Jeffrey was an avid photographer and was considering making photography a career.

"Hmm." Jeffrey grew thoughtful. Then he smiled at Elizabeth. "Sounds like a lot of work but it'll be fun."

Elizabeth nodded, already thinking about script ideas. "I know I can write a good script. . . ." Absorbed in thought, Elizabeth stared out across the beach. Gradually she became aware of the figure in her line of vision: Jessica.

"Hey, Jess!" Elizabeth shouted.

Yawning, Jessica looked up from her fashion magazine. "Yeah?"

"Jess, I have this great idea, and I want you to help."

Jessica's eyes darted to Jeffrey and then back to her twin. "Yeah?" she prompted. Lila hitched herself up on one elbow to listen.

With a quick glance at Jeffrey for encouragement, Elizabeth filled her sister in. "I was thinking about making a documentary on Sweet Valley—and you can help out, if you want to. It'll be fun. It's for a big showcase that Susan's father is organizing."

Jessica's face instantly assumed an expression of reluctant apology. "*Gee*, Liz. It sounds great. But I don't think I have the time." She shrugged with unconvincing regret. "Sorry."

A slow smile spread across Elizabeth's face. She knew her sister only too well. Anything that sounded remotely like work was to be avoided at all cost. Especially if it didn't seem to have any direct payoff—like money, or a boy, or some other worthwhile prize.

Suddenly Elizabeth had an idea. "Well, what I was hoping," she said casually, "was that you would want to be the narrator for the whole thing—on camera, I mean. But if you can't, I understand." As she turned away, she gave Jeffrey a surreptitious wink.

"Wait a second, Liz. Just what do you mean—that bit about 'on camera'?"

Hiding a smile, Elizabeth replied, "Well, what I thought was that you would be a kind of tour guide of Sweet Valley. You could read the script, and the camera would follow you all over town as you showed off the different places I wanted to film. That's all."

Jessica lowered her eyes and drew little circles in the sand in front of her with one finger. "Oh. Well—hey, you know what?" she said with exaggerated brightness. She looked up at her sister. "I just remembered I'm not going to be so busy after all. I was going to be tied up with this—um"—she darted a quick glance at Lila for inspiration—"with something for Lila," she continued, ignoring Lila's look of surprise. "But we aren't doing it after all. Right, Lila?"

"Oh. Yeah, right," Lila said quickly as Jessica nudged her with one foot. "I changed my mind. We're not doing it."

Jessica turned back to her sister with a brilliant smile. "See? So I guess I *can* be in your film after all, Liz. I think it's a great idea. When do we start?"

Elizabeth's control broke, and she fell onto her back, laughing. "Jessica," she called out, "you'll be perfect. You're a born actress."

Her twin smiled sheepishly. "Yeah, I guess I am, huh?"

*   *   *

Two hours later, Elizabeth and Jessica walked into the Wakefields' spacious, Spanish-tiled kitchen.

"Want something to drink?" Jessica asked, opening the refrigerator.

Elizabeth shook her head and grabbed a notepad from the counter. Sitting at the kitchen table, she quickly jotted down the ideas they had come up with on the beach. She didn't want to risk forgetting any of them.

"Do you think I should get a new outfit?" Jessica sat down across from her and took a sip from her can of diet soda. "Something reporterish."

"Hmm. Sure." Lost in thought, Elizabeth paid little attention to what her twin was saying.

"Or maybe I could wear your white linen suit, huh?"

Elizabeth gave Jessica a slightly sour look. Her twin had twice the number of clothes she had but found it necessary to raid Elizabeth's closet at least once a week. But if it would make Jessica enthusiastic about the project, it was a worthwhile sacrifice. "All right, Jess."

Mrs. Wakefield opened the door and stepped inside. She had been swimming in the pool in the backyard and was drying her blond hair with a towel. With her slim build and youthful, attractive features, Alice Wakefield was some-

31

times mistaken for the twin's older sister. "How was the beach, girls?"

"Good, Mom. Liz and I are making a documentary."

"Oh, really?" Giving Elizabeth a quizzical look, Mrs. Wakefield pulled out a chair, put the towel on the seat, and sat down.

Elizabeth explained. "It's about Sweet Valley. It's for a state-wide showcase—"

"And lots of important people will be looking at it," Jessica broke in. "I'm going to be the star of it, too."

"Somehow that doesn't surprise me, Jessica," Mrs. Wakefield said. She sent Elizabeth a wry grin. "What did she promise to do for you in return for her shot at stardom?"

"I'll invite her to my house in Malibu, even when I'm disgustingly rich and famous," Jessica retorted. She tossed her head and narrowed her eyes at her twin. "But only if she's *really* nice to me from now on."

"I'll keep that in mind," Elizabeth replied dryly. "Listen, I'm going to call Enid. I know she'll want to help. She's been talking a lot about video lately. Her mother's boyfriend works in TV—he's with the Sweet Valley station—and she's become pretty interested in television."

"That's a good idea, Liz." Mrs. Wakefield pushed herself up from the table and stretched luxuriously. "Twenty more laps, and I'll treat myself to an ice-cream sundae."

Elizabeth smiled and went to the phone. She quickly dialed the Rollinses' number, and Enid answered after a couple of rings.

"Hi, Enid. It's me. Listen, I've got this great idea. Remember that article I read to you yesterday about that documentary contest?"

"I knew it," Enid said smugly. "Go on. What's it going to be?"

"How does 'This Is Sweet Valley' grab you?"

Enid was silent for a minute, considering. "You know," she said slowly, "that could be really good."

Brimming with excitement, Elizabeth asked, "So? Want to help?"

"Absolutely!"

"Great. Lila said we could use her video camera, and Jeffrey will do most of the shooting. I'm writing a script, and Jess is going to be the narrator. But I want you to help out with everything, Enid. You always have such good ideas, and I'll need your creative inspiration."

"Sure. It really sounds—hold on a second, Liz. My grandmother's calling." There was a pause, and Elizabeth could hear muffled talking. Then Enid was back, sounding rushed. "Listen, I'll have to talk to you later. Bye."

There was a click, and the phone went dead in Elizabeth's hands. She stared at it, and then shrugged. "I hope it's nothing serious," she said to herself.

Enid raced downstairs, her feet pounding on the steps. "What is it, Nana? What's wrong?" Breathless, she ran into the kitchen.

Mrs. Langevin was standing in the middle of the room with a casserole dish in her hand. "Dear, I want to be useful around the house, so I'm putting away the clean dishes." She indicated the dishwasher with a nod. "But I don't know where this is supposed to go."

Enid heaved a sigh of relief and took the casserole from her grandmother's hands. "Up in this cupboard, above the stove, Nana. I'll put it away for you. But really, you don't have to do that," she added hastily as Mrs. Langevin pulled out the top rack and picked up a glass.

"No, no, no. I don't want to be a bother to you and Adele, Enid."

A thought flashed across Enid's mind: if her grandmother didn't want to be a bother, she could have waited until Enid was off the phone instead of calling her so urgently—just for a dish. But Enid dismissed the thought immediately as selfish and ungrateful. It was sweet of her grandmother to be so concerned about helping.

"OK, Nana," she said contritely. "I'll help you."

Her grandmother caught Enid's hand in a warm clasp. "You're such a good girl."

Enid blushed, ashamed at having such guilty thoughts. She smiled shakily. "It's only because I love you so much, Nana."

Mrs. Langevin patted her hand and gave her a loving smile in return. "I know you do, Enid. Maybe after you finish putting these dishes away, you can help me unpack?"

"Of course, Nana. Whatever you say."

Four

At six o'clock there was a knock on the Rollinses' door.

"That's probably Richard, honey," Mrs. Rollins called out from the kitchen. "Let him in, will you? I've got my hands full."

Richard Cernak had been Mrs. Rollins's boyfriend for the past six months. Enid thought he was nice enough, but she found it difficult to accept anyone as a possible replacement for her father, and she couldn't quite make up her mind whether she liked Richard or not. Wrinkling her nose, she reached for the door.

"Hi, Richard." She stepped aside as he gave her a friendly smile.

"Hi, Enid. Everything go OK at the airport

this morning?" he asked in an undertone, glancing in the direction of the living room.

She shrugged. She always had a hard time talking to him. "The flight was a bit late, but that's nothing unusual."

"No, I guess not."

"Hello, Richard!" Adele Rollins said as she came in from the kitchen. "Come on in and meet Mother. I've told her all about you."

Enid trailed behind as her mother and Richard went into the living room. Perching on the arm of the sofa, she watched her grandmother's reaction. It might have been her imagination, but Enid thought her grandmother appeared somewhat aloof and unfriendly.

"How do you do, Mr. Cernak?" Mrs. Langevin said with a touch of coolness in her voice.

"Please call me Richard." He settled back in an armchair and smiled pleasantly.

"We'll be eating in a few minutes," Adele Rollins said with a quick, affectionate glance at him.

He returned her smile. "Great. I've got to be at the studio later, so the sooner the better. Well," he continued, turning to Mrs. Langevin as Mrs. Rollins excused herself, "I hear your flight was delayed. Happens every time, right?"

"That hardly makes it more bearable for an old woman," Mrs. Langevin retorted.

Enid blinked and looked quickly at Richard. His smile wavered for an instant, but he shrugged off his surprise. "No, I suppose not. But I know you'll be comfortable now. Adele and Enid have been working very hard to make everything perfect for you. How do you like Sweet Valley so far? Think you'll be happy here?"

Mrs. Langevin didn't say anything. She just stared fixedly at the wall.

"Nana, how about some cheese and crackers?" Enid said quickly. She jumped up for the tray, wondering if her grandmother might be going slightly deaf in her old age.

But Mrs. Langevin beamed at her happily. "Thank you, dear. How kind of you."

As Enid passed the plate to Richard, she caught a questioning look from him. She gave him a tiny shrug.

"How's everything going?" Mrs. Rollins asked as she joined them. "Richard, how about a drink?"

"Thanks, Adele. Bourbon." As Mrs. Rollins went back into the kitchen, he turned to Enid's grandmother again. "So, I bet it's a lot warmer out here than it was back in Chicago, hmm? It's always sunny and warm in Sweet Valley."

"I never minded the cold."

Richard cast Enid another quick look, but Enid was concentrating on her grandmother. It was obvious that for some reason Mrs. Langevin didn't like Richard.

Enid studied her mother's boyfriend. He was an attractive man—in good shape, with dark, wavy hair graying slightly at his temples. He played a lot of tennis, so he had a good tan. He was dressed casually in chinos and a blue polo shirt. He wasn't remarkable one way or another, but there was clearly something about him her grandmother didn't like, and that made Enid suspicious. She eyed him doubtfully as her mother handed him a glass of bourbon.

"Thanks, Adele." He smiled gratefully at her, and she sat down in another chair.

"Mother, Richard works at the local television station, and he's offered to take you on a tour of the studios sometime."

"No. I don't think so." Mrs. Langevin sniffed and pulled her white cardigan closer around her shoulders. With a pointed glance at Richard's short-sleeved polo shirt, she added, "Dear, would you please close the window? I'm feeling the draft."

"It's eighty degrees outside," Richard said with an attempt at a hearty laugh.

But Enid's grandmother crossed her arms across her chest. "Unfortunately, old people feel the cold. Nobody seems to care, but that's the way it is."

"I—" Flustered, Richard broke off and took a long sip of his drink.

"Mother, he didn't mean anything by it," Adele Rollins said hurriedly. She stood up to close the window and smiled nervously at Richard. "Rich, can you give me a hand in the kitchen for a minute?"

"Sure." He set his glass down with a sharp click on the coffee table and followed Mrs. Rollins out of the room.

"Nana, what's wrong?" Enid whispered.

Mrs. Langevin darted a sharp look at Enid. "I don't like that man. I don't trust him."

"Why?" Enid bit her lower lip in consternation.

"Well, for one thing, I think he asks too many personal questions," her grandmother said in a hoarse whisper. She cast a glance in the direction of the kitchen. "And the way he drinks—didn't you notice? I think he's probably an alcoholic."

"Nana—I . . ." Enid regarded her grandmother. Mrs. Langevin was much older than Enid; surely she must be a more experienced judge of character. Maybe her grandmother was right.

"And another thing," Mrs. Langevin went on. She leaned closer to Enid. "The way he orders Adele around." Nodding wisely, she added, "He seems to expect her to do things for him—such as getting that drink."

"I never thought of it that way," Enid mused.

Her mind darted back to her mother rushing to the door and pouring Richard a drink, and a hundred other little things she had seen her mother do for him in the past. Her jaw clenched, and she began to feel a spark of anger.

Her grandmother nodded again and gave a sad little chuckle. "I guess you think I'm just a nosy old busybody."

"Of course not, Nana."

Mrs. Langevin shrugged slightly. "I'm just concerned about your mother, dear, that's all. I'd hate to see her get hurt—" She raised a warning finger as Richard and Mrs. Rollins came back in.

"Well, dinner's on the table," Mrs. Rollins said brightly. "Shall we?"

"May I?" Richard stepped forward to help Mrs. Langevin to her feet, but she looked pointedly at Enid and held out her arm.

Jumping up, Enid hurried to her grandmother's side. She heard Richard sigh and felt a flash of irritation. What right did he have to get annoyed just because Nana wanted *her* to help?

Throughout dinner, Adele Rollins and Richard kept up a casual conversation about their jobs, and Enid toyed with her food. She could feel the tension around the table, and she knew it was the result of her grandmother's attitude. She reacted hostilely every time Richard spoke to her.

"Adele tells me you're a champion baker," he said at one point.

Mrs. Langevin looked at him coldly, then turned to her daughter. "Adele, may I please have the salt and pepper? No." she continued. "Not anymore."

"Oh. I see. Well, I guess we all change, don't we?"

Enid had to admit she felt a little sorry for Richard. Even though her grandmother didn't like him, she didn't need to make it so obvious. But Enid also felt a growing sense of resentment against Richard.

By the time they got to dessert, there was an uncomfortable silence around the dinner table. As soon as he had finished, Richard glanced at his watch and put down his napkin. "Adele, I hate to eat and run, but I've got to get to the station now."

"No problem, Rich," Mrs. Rollins said hastily. Her forehead was creased with strain, and her jaw was set firmly. She stood up to follow him out of the room.

Setting down her teacup, Mrs. Langevin nodded curtly at Enid. "No manners. What did I tell you?"

Enid licked the last morsel of cake off her fork and frowned. Suddenly she felt more confused about Richard than ever.

* * *

"Where are you going, dear?" Enid's grandmother asked her the next afternoon.

Enid poked her head in the living room. Her grandmother was sitting by the window, flipping through a magazine.

"I've got a date, Nana. I usually try to spend Sunday afternoons with Hugh because he goes to a different school and we don't see each other every day," she explained quickly, listening for the sound of Hugh's car.

She heard a motor idling out front and gave her grandmother a cheerful wave. "Bye, Nana. See you later." Then she ran out the door to the curb, where Hugh's car was waiting.

"Hi," she said breathlessly, sliding into the front seat.

"Hi, yourself," he teased, giving her a wink.

She grinned back at him, and a tingle of happiness darted through her. She hadn't seen Hugh for a whole week. Eagerly she drank in every familiar feature, from his wavy brown hair to the cleft in his strong chin. She often found herself looking at him lately, as though she needed to reassure herself that he was still there, still the same Hugh. "Where should we go today?"

"How about Miller's Point?"

She raised her eyebrows as he pulled out into the traffic. "In the middle of the afternoon?"

she teased. Miller's Point was a popular evening spot. On any given night, there were generally ten or twelve cars parked up on the high bluff.

"Why not?" Hugh answered. "I hear there's a good view from up there, even though I've never seen it."

Enid chuckled and snuggled closer to him. "All right, let's go."

As they drove, Hugh said, "Listen, Big Mesa has an overnight camping trip to the desert every year. It's next weekend. Want to go?"

Instantly Enid pictured herself and Hugh sitting by a crackling campfire under a starry desert sky. It sounded exactly like the sort of thing that would get their relationship back on solid ground. There had been too many arguments lately about the time they had together—and where they spent it.

The previous weekend they had planned on going to the beach: Enid assumed they would go to the Sweet Valley beach and be with her friends, but Hugh wanted to go to the beach farther north, where his friends hung out. For some reason, that disagreement had escalated into a major conflict. And the week before, Hugh had had to cancel a date because of a last-minute surprise party for a classmate, someone Enid didn't even know. It seemed that finding time for each other was getting harder and harder to do.

But a camping trip out in the wild, the two of them together—it would be ideal. She closed her eyes, treasuring the daydream.

"Absolutely," she breathed.

"Will it be OK with your Mom?" Hugh asked, as he turned the car up the hill toward Miller's Point. "There are three teachers going, too."

"Sure. Mom knows you're a gentleman," Enid said. She gave him a playful dig in the ribs, and he chuckled as he pulled onto the grass and turned off the engine. "Besides, she's always saying how much she likes the desert herself, so I'm sure she'll be excited for me."

"Great. How are things going with your grandmother?"

Enid's face clouded over, but she gave herself a little shake. In a few days, Nana would be settled in, and things would go smoothly, she told herself firmly. She smiled at Hugh. "Fine. It'll work out fine. It's really great to have her around."

"Hey—this is pretty nice up here, you know?" Hugh turned to the view, his eyes twinkling as he put one arm across her shoulders.

"Hmm . . . you know, you're right." Enid laughed. Through the windshield they had an uninterrupted view of Sweet Valley and in the distance was the glittering blue Pacific.

"I've missed you," Hugh murmured, tightening his arm around her.

Enid caught her breath. "Me, too." She turned to look at him, a tender smile on her face. "I think next weekend will be wonderful. I can't wait."

"Let's get out. I brought a blanket and a new book I want to show you." He twisted around in the seat, to reach into the back. Then he gave her a playful grin and nodded toward the door. "Madame?"

With a happy laugh, Enid followed him and helped him spread out the blanket.

She and Hugh had discovered they had the same taste in books, and they often shared poems and passages from their favorite novels. As the sun beat down on them, Enid and Hugh took turns reading aloud from a book of Edward Lear's nonsense poems. But after half an hour, Hugh glanced at his watch, and his expression clouded. "It's time to go."

"So soon?" Enid felt crushed. "Do we have to?"

"Sorry. I told some friends I'd help them put up posters for the school play," he replied, jumping up.

"But, Hugh—" Enid bit her lip as she rose to her feet. Hugh began shaking out the blanket. "Why did you make plans with friends you can see at school? The weekend is the only time we can be together."

47

He let out his breath slowly. "Enid, I'm sorry, but I have other friends, too, you know, and stuff I should do at Big Mesa."

Enid turned away. She drew a deep breath, trying to control her feelings. If there was one thing she wanted to avoid, it was another argument about their time together. "OK," she said softly. "I understand."

The drive back down was completely quiet, and soon they had pulled up in front of Enid's house. Hugh turned off the engine, and they sat in silence for a moment.

"Hugh, I—"

"Enid—"

They both laughed awkwardly, and Enid shook her head. "Sorry, Hugh. I didn't mean to be so crabby back there."

With a tender smile, he took her hand again. "You weren't. Forget it."

"I'll talk to you later, OK?"

"Right." Hugh leaned forward and kissed her softly.

Impulsively, Enid put her arms around his neck and held him tightly for a moment, then broke away. "See you on Friday." Smiling she opened the door and got out. Hugh started the engine and pulled away.

As Enid turned to walk up to the house, she saw her grandmother standing at the window, peeking out. Then the curtain was moved back into place. She realized after a second that her grandmother's expression had been stern and disapproving.

Enid frowned, puzzled. There was no reason for Nana to disapprove of her and Hugh. But in spite of herself, she felt a twinge of worry.

Five

"I still don't see why we have to go to Enid's for this strategy meeting," Jessica said, as Elizabeth drove toward the Rollinses' house after school on Monday. Enid had never been one of Jessica's favorite people.

"I've told you a dozen times, Jess," Elizabeth replied. "Enid's grandmother only got here two days ago, and Enid didn't want to leave her all alone so soon."

"Well, what's wrong with her? Is she sick or something?"

"No, Enid just thinks it would be nice for her to have some company, that's all."

"Yeah, but still—it's *our* documentary, right?" Jessica insisted. "Enid should be meeting us at our house."

Elizabeth sighed in exasperation. Jessica never got tired of letting her know how little she liked Enid.

"*Jessica*—"

"Just asking, that's all," Jessica interrupted airily. Elizabeth shook her head as she parked the car in front of the house. "Come on."

At the same moment, Jeffrey drove up behind them, and the three walked up to the front door together.

"Come on in, you guys," Enid said. She gave them a slightly apologetic shrug, adding, "I hope you don't mind, but I told my grandmother she could sit in on the meeting. I guess it's kind of boring for her all alone all day."

"Of course we don't mind," Elizabeth said quickly, sensing Enid's embarrassment. She caught a pained look from her sister and frowned a warning at her.

"Sure," Jeffrey added gallantly. "It's fine with me."

Enid smiled and closed the door behind them. "Thanks. Well, come on in. Nana," she called as she led them into the living room. "Nana, these are my friends Liz and Jessica Wakefield and Jeffrey French."

Mrs. Langevin smiled pleasantly at them from the sofa, and Elizabeth walked forward, her hand outstretched.

"Mrs. Langevin, I'm very glad to meet you. Enid's told me so much about you."

52

Mrs. Langevin looked past her at Jessica and gave her an inquiring look. It was the look they always got at first meeting, and Elizabeth smiled. "Yes, we're identical twins. I'm Liz."

"Isn't that nice, dear. And what is this meeting about?"

"Well," Elizabeth began, taking a seat near the older woman, "we're making a documentary about Sweet Valley. I'm writing the script, my sister is narrating, Jeffrey is the camera crew, and Enid is my all-around indispensable adviser on everything," she finished, her eyes twinkling.

"Why don't we sit around the coffee table so we can write things down," Enid suggested. "Or we could go into the dining room."

"Oh, I'm sure we'll all be comfortable here, dear," her grandmother said with a smile. Enid nodded absently.

Taking the lead, Elizabeth outlined her plan. "I'm pretty sure about all the things I want to include," she began. She tucked a lock of hair behind one ear. "And I think the first thing we should do is start with the history of Sweet Valley."

"This sounds like a barrel of laughs," Jessica muttered, resting her chin in one hand.

Jeffrey laughed. "You can make it dramatic, Jess. Don't worry."

"It's just a short introduction, Jess. We'll go

right into the good stuff from there, don't worry. We'll get the mayor, some local celebrities for you to interview."

As she jotted down notes, Elizabeth heard Enid's grandmother clear her throat, and she looked up politely. "Do you have any suggestions, Mrs. Langevin? What do you think would be interesting to know about Sweet Valley that we could include?"

"Oh, don't mind me," the woman replied. "I'll just sit here quietly and not get in your way." She peered intently at her watch, then said to Enid, "Dear, it's three-thirty."

Enid looked perplexed. "Yes? Oh, right—your tea, Nana. I'll go make it right now."

Her grandmother beamed with satisfaction. "Thank you, dear. You're so sweet."

As Enid jumped up and left the room, the others sat quietly around the coffee table with Enid's grandmother. She smiled pleasantly at them and tugged her cardigan around her shoulders.

"So . . ." Jeffrey said with a bright smile. He looked around, and Elizabeth met his eye, trying not to let her embarrassment show. Having Enid's grandmother there put a curb on their spontaneity, and none of them seemed to know what to say while Enid was gone. Jessica sighed heavily and pulled a pocket mirror out of her shoulder bag to check her lip gloss.

"Here, Nana," Enid said, hurrying back a few minutes later with a steaming mug. "So, what did I miss?"

"Not much," Jessica drawled sarcastically.

"Anyway," Elizabeth put in quickly, "I think we should start shooting downtown tomorrow."

Jessica shook her head. "Nope, sorry. Cheerleading tomorrow."

"Well, Wednesday, then, right after school." Elizabeth turned to the others. "Is that all right with everyone?"

Enid looked at her grandmother. "You won't mind, will you, Nana? I'll be gone most of the afternoon."

"No, dear," Mrs. Langevin said, her voice suddenly faint and weary. Only a moment ago she had sounded firm and decisive. Her hand fluttered up to her heart in a dramatic gesture. "I don't mind."

Elizabeth felt the smile freeze on her face as Enid's expression went from hope to worry and guilt. Clearly, her friend was upset at the idea of leaving her grandmother alone.

As they made up a list of locations for shooting, Elizabeth listened to the quiet conversation between Enid and Mrs. Langevin. It was only natural that her best friend loved her grandmother and was very concerned about her. But it almost seemed to Elizabeth that Mrs. Langevin was taking advantage of Enid's generous good nature, asking her to go get her things and making little complaints, such as about the temperature of the tea. And Enid's discomfort affected the others, too. By the time they were ready to wrap up the discussion, they were all a little uneasy.

"Is everything all right, Enid?" Elizabeth asked as they headed for the door.

A shadow passed across Enid's face, but it was gone in an instant. "Yeah, fine. By the way, I'm going on an overnight next weekend with Hugh—a school trip of his. I think it'll really help things with us."

Elizabeth put her hand on Enid's arm and squeezed. "That sounds great. I want to hear more about it. See you tomorrow."

With a preoccupied nod, Enid turned away. "Yeah. Bye."

"Man, Enid's grandmother is a real pain," Jessica stated bluntly as she got into the Fiat.

"Jessica!" Elizabeth exclaimed. "How can you say that?"

"I don't know. I just can. There's something about that woman I don't like."

Elizabeth thought about how awkward and uncomfortable Enid had seemed. But surely it was because Mrs. Langevin had just arrived in Sweet Valley. The situation had to improve, didn't it?

*   *   *

Wednesday afternoon Elizabeth pushed her locker door shut and checked to see if she had everything she needed. Tucked securely in her bag was the script she had been working on since Sunday afternoon. She nodded, satisfied.

"Hi,'" Enid said as Jeffrey sauntered up. "Are we all set?"

"The star is in the girls' room, fixing her makeup," Elizabeth said dryly. Glancing up at Jeffrey, she added, "And make sure you always shoot her from her best side."

"How about I just shoot her, period?" he offered, looking hopeful.

Elizabeth punched him playfully on the arm.

"OK, here I am," Jessica announced suddenly. She executed a stately pirouette for their admiration. She had changed from her school clothes into Elizabeth's white linen suit and a bright blue blouse. "How do I look?"

"Hmm . . ." Elizabeth murmured. She moved closer to Enid, and the two of them examined Jessica for a long moment.

Jessica shook her head impatiently. "Oh, no, you don't. You go through this every time I ask, and I'm not falling for it this time." She headed for the door. "Come on, let's go."

Elizabeth looked at Enid and Jeffrey and shrugged. "The royal summons, I guess."

In minutes they were heading downtown in Jeffrey's car. As they approached the building where the twins' father, Ned Wakefield, had his law office, Elizabeth said, "Oh, Jeffrey, stop here. It's a good central location."

"OK," Jeffrey replied, pulling the car to the side of the road. "Let me walk around for a few minutes to check out the good camera angles and buildings." He reached into the backseat for Lila's video camera and them climbed out.

Elizabeth dug into her bag. "Here, Jess. This is the finished script. I changed some things, so why don't you look it over for a few minutes."

Jessica took the script and began studying it, and Elizabeth and Enid walked a short distance away. From the expression on Enid's face, Elizabeth could tell she was very preoccupied.

"Hey, is something wrong?" she asked softly.

They stopped in front of a store window and Enid let out a deep breath. "I don't know—I—" She shook her head. "I guess Nana is pretty old-fashioned, but she saw Hugh kiss me good-bye the other day, and she keeps bringing it up with Mom, like it was really improper or something."

"Oh, well, she'll get used to it. I know she will," Elizabeth said, trying to sound reassuring.

Just then Jeffrey walked up to them. "All ready," he declared.

After a sympathetic smile at Enid, Elizabeth turned to Jessica, who was leaning against the car, studying the script.

"OK, Jessica," Elizabeth called out to her twin. "Do you think you know your lines?"

"Yes, Liz. I'm ready. Where do we start?"

Jeffrey hoisted the camera onto his shoulder and nodded toward the steps of the town hall. "Over there. And then we can come back when we tape your interview with the mayor."

Smoothing down her skirt, Jessica set off for the steps. When she turned around, she wore a serious but friendly expression, and she nodded at Jeffrey. "I'm ready."

Elizabeth, Enid, and Jeffrey all looked at one another expectantly, and Elizabeth laughed with excitement. "All right—I guess this is it! Let's go for it!"

"Welcome to Sweet Valley, California," Jessica began smoothly. "It's a small town, a quiet town, and maybe a lot like your own hometown. But Sweet Valley has a life and a character all its own. . . ."

"She's doing a nice job." Enid murmured later as Jeffrey followed Jessica down the sidewalk.

Elizabeth nodded, her eyes fixed on her twin. Jessica *was* doing a nice job, and Elizabeth felt a surge of pride in her sister.

Elizabeth tried to concentrate on the filming, but out of the corner of her eye, something caught her attention. She turned quickly to see Winston Egbert stepping out of a novelty shop with a fake arrow through his head. He acted quite nonchalant, pausing to look into store windows, but he gradually caught up to Jessica and walked along behind her as she talked.

Clamping a hand to her mouth, Elizabeth started giggling and grabbed Enid by the arm. As soon as Enid turned, she saw and started laughing, too.

Elizabeth dragged Enid along with her as she ran to catch up with Jeffrey and Jessica—and Winston. She could see Jeffrey smiling and trying to hold the camera steady, but it was clear that Jessica had no idea what was going on behind her.

As the procession moved down the sidewalk, people stopped to watch, pointing and grinning. Jessica, who thought they were admiring her, smiled dazzlingly. But as more and more people followed them and began laughing, her smile became slightly fixed. Finally she stopped and turned around. Her face burned pink.

"Winston!"

Elizabeth and Enid collapsed in gales of laughter, clutching at each other for support. Soon the crowd of onlookers dispersed, and Jeffrey continued to tape Jessica's harangue at Winston, who maintained a serene smile, as he looked innocently up at the sky.

"Jeffrey, erase that tape this instant," Jessica fumed when she realized what he was doing.

He looked past her and caught Elizabeth's eye. "OK, Jess," he said. "See," he continued, poking at a button. "I'm rewinding it, and when we tape again, it will erase. All right?"

Quivering with indignation, Jessica let out a deep breath. "All right. And if you ever do that again, Win," she added, turning on Winston, "I will put a real arrow through your head."

"You didn't really rewind it, did you?" Elizabeth whispered, coming up behind Jeffrey. He gave her with an impish grin and silently shook his head. With a laugh, Elizabeth squeezed his arm. "Great. OK, Jess? Come on, our appointment with the mayor is in fifteen minutes. Ready?"

Instantly, Jessica was all smiles again. It was clear she wasn't going to let anything ruin her shot at stardom. "Ready when you are," she said airily and led the way back to the town hall.

Six

"The mayor was so funny," Elizabeth said, as she, Jessica, and Jeffrey followed Enid up to her front door later that afternoon. "He's even more of a ham than Jessica."

"Oh, thanks a lot," Jessica protested. "He's *way* out of my league, I'll have you know. I hardly got to say anything at all during the whole stupid interview."

They all laughed, as Enid led the way into the house. She walked into the living room and froze. On the sofa, her grandmother was stretched out with a crocheted afghan pulled up to her chin. The others were still chattering behind her as she pulled up shortly, and Mrs. Langevin opened her eyes with a start.

"Oh, Nana! Sorry," Enid gasped, stepping

backward into her friends. The laughter trickled into silence as Elizabeth, Jeffrey, and finally Jessica realized they had just disturbed the old woman's afternoon nap.

"That's quite all right," Mrs. Langevin said, sounding as if it wasn't right at all. She pushed herself up into a sitting position and pressed her lips tightly together.

"We're awfully sorry, Mrs. Langevin," Elizabeth said. She looked at the others. "I guess we'd better go."

Enid swallowed and glanced nervously at her friends. "Sorry. Thanks for dropping me off. I'll talk to you tomorrow."

Jeffrey, Elizabeth, and Jessica silently followed Enid as she led the way back to the door. Waving feebly, she closed it after them. All her satisfaction about their first day of taping had quickly disappeared, replaced by guilt. She hurried back to the living room.

"I'm really sorry, Nana. I—we didn't know—"

"You know, Enid, I'm not sure your friends are the nicest young people for you to be spending time with," Mrs. Langevin announced peevishly, shaking out the afghan.

Enid blinked. "Wh-what do you mean?"

"Noisy, rambunctious—and rather inconsiderate, too, I might add, bursting in on me like that."

"Oh, but, Nana, they didn't know you were—"

Her grandmother held up a hand. "I thought so the other day when they were here, too, but I didn't want to say anything then. Especially that Liz. She seems very bossy to me, ordering everyone around."

"She's not like that at all!" Enid protested in surprise. Elizabeth Wakefield was the last person Enid would ever consider bossy. She had to make her grandmother understand that. "Liz is the sweetest, nicest person in the whole world, Nana. Once you get to know her—" She broke off, hearing the front door open and shut.

"Hi, Mother, hi, Enid," Mrs. Rollins said as she came in, briefcase in hand. "How was your day, Mother?"

Mrs. Langevin shrugged. "Oh, it was fine, Adele. Just fine."

"Great. Enid, can I talk to you for a minute? Excuse us for a moment, Mother."

"Sure," Enid said, wondering what her mother wanted.

"Enid," Mrs. Rollins began when they were in the kitchen. "I told Richard I'd have dinner with him tonight, so would you mind staying in?"

Enid felt a spark of irritation, and she sat down at the table, not looking at her mother. "Do you have to go out with him tonight?"

"What is that supposed to mean?"

Enid shrugged.

"Look at me please, Enid," her mother said sharply. Enid raised her chin defiantly. "What's wrong?"

"I just don't see why you can't stay home with your own mother," Enid shot back angrily. "Not that I mind, but why do I have to keep her happy all the time?"

"Enid, that's not fair, and you know it."

Enid picked up the saltshaker and toyed with it. Then she muttered, "Well, I don't exactly think it's fair that it's my free time that gets used up first, that's all. What if I had had a date with Hugh tonight or something?"

"Well, you don't, do you?"

Stung, Enid shook her head. The question hurt, not because her mother meant it to, but because it reminded her of how bad things were with Hugh. Well, at least the weekend should turn things around.

For a moment her mother stared at her speechlessly. Then, with a sigh of exasperation, she left the room. Enid felt her shoulders sag suddenly, as though a heavy weight had been loaded onto her back. She slumped in her chair and stared at the wall.

Later, over dinner, her grandmother brought up the subject of Enid's friends again. "You know, dear. I really have to wonder about this movie thing you've gotten involved in. It seems like a big waste of time. I was all alone all afternoon while you were out."

Enid ducked her head. Her grandmother wasn't being completely fair, but Enid didn't know how to tell her that. "I'm sorry, Nana," she said slowly, trying hard not to sound angry. "I didn't know I'd be gone so long."

"And I thought we were going to make our afternoon tea a tradition."

"Tomorrow, Nana. I promise." Nana might be exaggerating the situation, but Enid felt terrible. Of course it would be lonely and boring for her grandmother to spend the whole afternoon by herself.

"And when you have time for your schoolwork is beyond me," Mrs. Langevin added. "These extra projects will make trouble for you, especially if they aren't worthwhile."

"Yes, Nana."

As Enid got up to clear the dishes, her anger at her mother returned. *If Mom was home more often, poor Nana wouldn't feel so lonely!* she thought. *It's all Mom's fault.*

On Friday morning Mrs. Rollins tapped lightly on Enid's door. "Can I talk to you for a minute?"

Enid looked up warily. The tone of her mother's voice indicted that she wasn't going to like what her mother had to say.

Mrs. Rollins drew a deep breath and faced Enid squarely. "Enid, I've been thinking about this overnight trip with Hugh—and I'm sorry honey, but I just don't like it."

"What do you mean?" Enid's voice was low.

"Mother and I have been talking about it, and I think I agree with her—I really don't think you should be out overnight with your boyfriend."

Enid felt as if the wind had been knocked out of her. She couldn't believe her mother was saying this! Clenching her hands together to keep them from shaking, she let her breath out slowly. "Mom," she said, forcing her voice to stay level, "you've always liked Hugh. You know he would never—"

"I'm sorry, Enid. That's just the way I feel. I may have been too lenient in the past, but now I'm putting my foot down. You'll just have to tell Hugh you can't go."

"But, Mom—"

Mrs. Rollins shook her head firmly and moved out into the hallway. "No, Enid. That's the end of the discussion. Now I've got to get to work. Oh, and by the way," she added, turning back, "Mother mentioned last night that she'd like to go to the library this afternoon—and since it's the first time she's shown any interest in going out, I'd really appreciate it if you could take her after school."

68

"But, Mom, I told Liz I'd help her on the movie this afternoon," Enid said, her voice desperate.

"Enid, this is your own *grandmother*. Really! Sometimes I'm surprised at you."

Enid turned away, pressing her lips together. This was getting to be too much, she thought angrily. "OK, Mom. I will."

"Enid, what's wrong?" Elizabeth asked when they met before homeroom in the crowded, noisy hallway.

Enid shook her head in utter disbelief. "Mom decided all of a sudden she doesn't trust Hugh, and now I can't go on the camping trip with him!"

"You're kidding!"

Enid shook her head again and leaned back against her locker. "No, I am definitely *not* kidding. Nana has the wrong impression about him, and I guess Mom started to believe her. I mean, Mom thought it would be fine with three teachers going, but I guess even that isn't enough now. I'm so furious with her. I don't know *how* I'm going to explain this to Hugh."

"Enid?" Elizabeth looked sideways at her, a doubtful expression on her face. "I don't mean to be critical or anything, but it sounds like it's your grandmother you should be furious

69

with, not your mom. Couldn't you explain to her?"

Enid shook her head. "No, it's not Nana—I mean, it's not really her fault," she insisted. "She just doesn't understand, but my mother should know better."

"Oh." Nodding uncertainly, Elizabeth took some books from her locker and tucked them under her arm. "Well—I guess you would know."

There was a short pause, and Enid stared at the floor. She could understand why Elizabeth though it was Nana's fault, but it wasn't as if her grandmother were doing it deliberately. Enid had to admit to herself, however, that even if it wasn't deliberate, Nana was causing trouble anyway.

"Oh, and another thing," Enid said, turning to her locker again and avoiding Elizabeth's gaze. "I can't help out this afternoon; I have to take Nana to the library."

Elizabeth was about to say something, but she stopped herself. "OK," she said finally, giving Enid a small smile. "I understand. But I'm sorry."

"Yeah. Me, too."

"Well, since you're not going away this weekend, will you be able to come to the beach tomorrow?" Elizabeth asked tentatively.

"I'll try," Enid said tersely. "But at this point I just don't know."

Enid slammed the telephone down. There was no answer at Hugh's house. She had tried to get him as soon as she got back from school, but no one was home. Then she had taken her grandmother to the library and waited for her to pick out some books. Enid had been trying his number ever since they got back, but without any luck. By now he was probably on his way over to pick her up for their weekend together.

She dropped down into a chair by a front window and stared out at the street. Shaking her head, she muttered, "I can't believe this is happening. It's so unfair."

Hugh's car pulled up at the curb, and Enid felt her stomach churning. She didn't know what she was going to say. Shaking her head in defeat, she rose and went to open the door.

"Hi," Hugh said, kissing her. "All ready to go?"

Enid's throat tightened as she looked at him. He was dressed for camping in jeans, hiking boots, and a plaid shirt. She shook her head, and his smile disappeared. A puzzled frown creased his forehead. "What is it? What's wrong?"

"I can't go."

He stared at her incredulously. "What do you mean, you can't go?"

"My mother told me this morning that she—she didn't want me to—"

"She can't trust me, right?" Hugh's eyes hardened. "Great. That's just great," he said in a bitter voice. "Thanks for letting me know."

"I couldn't—" Enid stopped and pulled herself together. She didn't want to start crying, but she was afraid she might. "I tried to call you after school," she said. "But then I had to take my grandmother to the library, and—"

"Couldn't you have taken her some other time? I think you could have tried a little harder to get through to me before I came over here to pick you up."

"Hugh!" Tears sprang to Enid's eyes. She didn't know what to say.

He looked away. "Listen, Enid. If you don't think you have time for this relationship, just say so. But personally, I don't know how much longer I can go on with a girlfriend I never see."

"I'm really sorry, Hugh," she repeated faintly, tears spilling down her cheeks. "I wish you would just try to understand, that's all."

"I understand, Enid. Believe me."

"Hugh!" She grabbed his arm and said desperately, "Listen—next weekend we'll do something really special, all right? I promise. It's just that adjusting to having my grandmother move in is taking longer than we thought, and—" She broke off and leaned against the doorframe.

Finally he nodded. "OK. I'm really disappointed, that's all."

"Me, too," she whispered. "You'd better go now—it's getting late."

"I guess so. Please, Enid, don't cry," he said, giving her a tender smile.

She nodded. "I'll be fine. Go on."

As Hugh climbed into his car and drove off, Enid saw her mother's car rounding the corner. She watched with icy calm as her mother parked and walked slowly to the house.

"Well, I'll be lucky if Hugh ever speaks to me again," Enid said as soon as her mother was within earshot. "And I wouldn't blame him."

Mrs. Rollins closed her eyes briefly as she climbed the steps to the door. "Listen, Enid. Let's not start this again," she said in a low voice. "I have told you what my feelings are about it, and that's the end of it."

"Well, what about my feelings?" Enid retorted, her voice rising indignantly. "Don't they count?"

"Enid!" Mrs. Rollins turned on her quickly. "*Please* keep your voice down. I don't want Mother to hear us bickering like this on the front steps—it would upset her."

Enid choked back a reply and glanced through the open doorway. It *would* upset Nana to hear them arguing, and she had said she was tired from going out, too. Drawing a shaky breath, Enid nodded, trying hard to swallow the lump in her throat.

"Now could we just have a quiet evening?" her mother asked in a tired voice. "We've been getting a little short with each other, and we could use a break."

Enid said nothing as she followed her mother into the house.

Seven

Elizabeth chewed on the end of her pen for a moment, lost in thought. At her feet, Prince Albert, the twins' golden retriever, slept in a shaft of morning sunlight. She glanced down at the dog with an absent smile. Then she turned to her journal again and continued writing.

I don't know what to do about Enid—or even if I should do anything at all. She seems so worried, and I get the feeling it has something to do with her grandmother. I know how much she loves her grandmother, so she should be happy that she's here. But obviously she isn't. Something is really bugging her, I can tell, even though she doesn't seem to want to talk about it.

75

Knowing Enid, she probably thinks she has to be loyal and pretend her grandmother is as perfect as she always thought. I'll definitely try to talk to her about it today, when we're at the beach.

"Liz! Which bathing suit should I wear?" Jessica demanded, popping her head through the door of the bathroom that connected their bedrooms. She held out two skimpy bikinis.

Lowering her pen, Elizabeth looked up. "Well, to tell you the truth," she said, squinting critically at the two suits, "I think you should probably wear a sun dress, or something a little more—substantial," she said.

Jessica came into the room wrapped in a towel and flopped down on Elizabeth's bed. "Are you trying to tell me something, Elizabeth Wakefield?"

"Just because we're filming on the beach doesn't mean you have to show off your gorgeous body," Elizabeth said with a chuckle.

"You don't want me to start a riot with all the hunks on the beach, right?" Jessica quipped.

Elizabeth snorted with amusement and snapped her journal shut. "How generous of you, Jess. Always thinking of others. Come on, we've got to get going. I've been waiting for you for twenty minutes." Dragging her sister firmly by the hand, Elizabeth led her into the other bedroom.

At first it was hard to decide which were Jessica's clean clothes and which were the dirty ones. Every surface was covered with shirts, skirts, sweaters, and dresses, and the closet stood gaping and empty. "Here, put this on," Elizabeth suggested, pulling a pink sun dress from the top of one relatively neat pile.

Jessica took it from her in stony silence and quickly slipped it on.

"Oh, girls," Mrs. Wakefield called, as the twins came downstairs. "Since you'll be at the beach all day, how about taking the dog with you? Give him a good workout and a swim in the ocean."

"Sure, Mom," Elizabeth said, resting her hand on his head. She smiled down at Prince Albert, and he wagged his tail excitedly. "Let's go."

Soon they were heading for the beach, the Saturday morning sun shining brightly down on the open convertible. Prince Albert blissfully leaned his head over the side, tongue out, ears flapping in the wind.

Jeffrey was waiting for the twins as they pulled up alongside his car in the public parking lot.

"Isn't Enid here yet?" Elizabeth asked.

He shrugged. "I haven't seen her. She knows what time we're starting, right?"

"Yes, I told her. Maybe we should wait a few minutes."

"Oh, come on!" Jessica exclaimed. "She doesn't have to be here just so we can start working, does she?"

They exchanged a quick glance, and Elizabeth's eyes flicked to her watch. They were fifteen minutes late already, and Enid was usually on time. Frowning, she shook her head. "OK, let's start. She'll probably show up later."

Elizabeth consulted her schedule. That day they were shooting the beach scenes, and the next week they were planning to cover a town meeting, the annual dance festival, and an interview with Sweet Valley's oldest living resident. She nodded firmly. "You're ready to talk about the art scene in Sweet Valley, aren't you, Jess?"

Jessica, who was touching up her makeup in the car's side mirror, nodded emphatically,. "Of course I am—I'm a professional." She straightened and gave them a brilliant smile. "Let's get to it." Then she led the way down the beach, Prince Albert loping at her side.

When they got to a row of deserted beach cabanas, they stopped, and Jessica squared her shoulders. "All right, roll 'em."

"I thought I was supposed to say that," Elizabeth teased, taking a seat on the sand. Jeffrey chuckled and toyed for a moment with the camera's focus. "Ready, Jeffrey?" she prompted softly. He nodded. "OK, then. Roll 'em."

As Jessica spoke about the artist colony that used to be located on the beaches of Sweet Valley, Elizabeth checked her watch and looked back down the beach. By now lots of students from Sweet Valley High were arriving, but there was still no sign of Enid.

With a melancholy sigh, Elizabeth turned back to her page of notes. Prince Albert went sniffing and snuffling off toward the cottages.

"What's next?" Jessica asked eagerly when Jeffrey had stopped the filming. "Interviews?"

From the beginning, Elizabeth had decided that a key feature of the documentary would be lots of interviews with Sweet Valley residents, all speaking to the camera about their feelings for the town.

"Yes. I think we should. But let Prince Albert go swimming first," she suggested.

As they headed down toward the water, a look of ecstasy appeared in Prince Albert's big brown eyes. He didn't often get to go to the beach, so when he did, he could hardly contain himself. For a few paces he walked sedately at their side, but then he bounded ahead and plunged joyfully into the surf.

Elizabeth and Jessica laughed as the dog

splashed around in the water, snorting salt out of his nose and shaking himself all over. When he had had enough, he came sloshing up out of the waves. He paused, dripping, with an expectant look on his face. Then, without warning, he came racing toward Jessica.

"*No!* Down, Albert, down!" she screamed, trying to get away from the sopping, leaping dog. Prince Albert obviously thought it was a game, and the more Jessica shrieked and ran away from him, the more boisterously he jumped around and chased her. Jessica's dress was clinging to her legs in dark wet patches, and water dribbled down her bare arms. "Get down, Albert!"

Laughing uncontrollably, Elizabeth noticed that Jeffrey had the camera up to his eye, and she laughed even harder. The incident would make a priceless piece of footage. Finally, she ran to the dog and grabbed him by the collar. "Albert, *down!*" she commanded. Instantly, Prince Albert sat back on his haunches, looked up at Elizabeth, and waited for further instructions.

"Oooh, I could die," Jessica groaned, pulling her sticky dress away from her. She darted a venomous look at her dog. "Why didn't you listen to me when *I* said it, huh?"

"At least you're not going on camera anymore today," Elizabeth said with a laugh. "We

80

just need you to interview people on the beach, and we won't be filming you."

A wary look crossed Jessica's face, and she glanced quickly at Jeffrey. He had the camera at his side and was looking innocently across the water. She shrugged. "Well . . . I guess so. Let's go, huh? We've got those interviews to do." With a glance over her shoulder she added, "And I promised some of the guys we would start with them."

"This is perfect," Elizabeth murmured later, watching the western horizon blaze pink and orange. Feeling contented, she leaned against Jeffrey's side. It had been a wonderful day. All the interviews on the beach had gone well, and they had taped many of their friends playing volleyball, lounging in the sun, and surfing. For scenes of a California town, their shots at the beach couldn't be beat.

Then Jessica had driven home with Prince Albert to get ready for a date, leaving Elizabeth and Jeffrey to enjoy the sunset. And now, a glorious sky finished off the day.

Jeffrey turned to Elizabeth and wrapped his arms around her. "I couldn't agree with you more," he whispered. "Just you and me and the deep blue sea."

"Mmm . . ." Closing her eyes happily, Elizabeth snuggled deeper into his side. But something kept intruding on the peace of the evening. She frowned and sat up.

"What is it?" Jeffrey asked gently brushing a wisp of hair from Elizabeth's forehead.

She sighed. "Enid. It's not that I'm angry or anything like that about her not coming today. It's just—well, why couldn't she come? It's not like her to cancel plans without any explanation."

"Are you worried about her?"

"I don't know. I'm probably just being oversensitive, that's all. I'm just—I guess I'm just disappointed for her. I know she was really excited about working on this documentary, but it's turning out that she isn't getting to do very much."

He tightened his arm around her. "Maybe she just changed her mind," he suggested, but he sounded unconvinced in spite of his reassuring hug.

"No. She'd tell me if she didn't *want* to help out."

They sat in silence for a few minutes as the last golden rays of the sun warmed their faces. It was a beautiful, serene Pacific sunset, but for Elizabeth, all the joy had gone out of it. She couldn't help thinking that her best friend was upset and troubled.

"Maybe she had to do something for her grandmother."

Elizabeth sighed again. "You're probably right. It probably has something to do with her grandmother." But that only made Elizabeth more certain than ever that there was more trouble at the Rollins house than Enid was willing to admit.

Eight

"Hi, honey, it's me," Mrs. Rollins said as Enid answered the phone Monday evening. "I'll be leaving work in a few minutes. Is there anything I should pick up at the store on my way home?"

"No."

The abruptness of Enid's answer sent a ripple of irritation through Mrs. Rollins. "Milk?" she prompted, trying to keep the hurt out of her voice. "Bread? Anything?"

"No, Mom." Enid sighed, then said, "I'll see you later."

"OK, honey. I'll be home soon." Mrs. Rollins lowered the telephone and stared moodily at the jumble of papers on her desk. There was a tight knot of anxiety lodged just above her stomach that had been growing for days. She tried to tell herself it was because of Enid. Ever since Friday, when she had told Enid she couldn't go on the field trip with Hugh, Enid had been keeping herself aloof. It had been three days now, and it was really beginning to bother her.

But she knew there was more to it than that. When she joined Richard later for dinner, he was going to expect an answer to his marriage proposal. Nearly a week had passed since he had asked her, and she still didn't know what to say. A few weeks earlier, she would have married him without a minute's hesitation. But now . . .

Now everything seemed confused and muddled. It wasn't that she didn't love him as much as ever, but her mother seemed to *dislike* him so much, which Mrs. Rollins simply couldn't understand. Her mother kept making pointed comments about him, and sarcastic asides to Enid. And now Enid was being hostile toward him, too, which made things even harder. Mrs. Rollins just didn't know what to do about it all, and she couldn't get used to the change in her mother's personality. It was throwing everything off-balance.

One of Mrs. Rollins's co-workers paused outside her office door to say good night. Her train of thought broken, she glanced at her watch:

five o'clock. Only two hours to go until she met Richard—and had to give him an answer.

Enid followed slowly behind her friends Elizabeth, Jeffrey, and Jessica as they hurried toward the local television station building the next afternoon. Elizabeth had scheduled an interview for that day with Jeremy Frank, the handsome host of "Frankly Speaking," a local talk show. Even though Enid was excited about meeting Jeremy Frank, there was a good chance that she might run into Richard Cernak, who was the station's program director. Richard was the one person she didn't feel like seeing. She knew what he and her mother had been arguing about on the front doorstep the night before, even though she couldn't quite catch all the words.

"I just don't know what to tell you right now, Rich," her mother had said in a tear-filled voice. "I really just need some time to let things settle down around here."

Richard's reply had been muffled, a low, unintelligible rumble. Enid's own heart had pounded like thunder in her ears. She knew she shouldn't have been eavesdropping, but she felt paralyzed by their conversation—there was no way on earth she could *not* listen.

"No! Let's just wait, please?" she had heard her mother say. "You *know* I love you, and I do want to be with you, but I just can't marry you right now. Can't you see that? Let's just leave things the way they are for a while." Then the door had opened and closed softly, and Mrs. Rollins hurried upstairs without saying a word.

"Come on, Enid," Elizabeth called to her excitedly now. "Don't be such a slowpoke."

Their eyes met. In spite of Elizabeth's joking mood, Enid could tell her friend was paying close attention to her, trying to figure out what was wrong. Could she just come right out and admit that ever since her grandmother's arrival, everything had gotten totally confused? No, it wasn't that way at all. Enid loved her grandmother, and she just had to make things work better. She made herself smile and jogged a few paces to catch up with the others on the building steps.

"Sorry. I was thinking about all the homework I have to do tonight," she lied. Stepping forward, she opened the heavy glass door and led the way to the elegant, plant-filled lobby.

"We're here to see Mr. Frank," Jessica announced as she walked up to the receptionist. "We have an appointment for four o'clock."

"Wakefield?" the woman asked, consulting a large appointment calendar. She looked up again and smiled at them. "Mr. Frank is expecting you in studio four. If you'll all sign in, I can give you some visitors' passes and show you the way."

Throwing a huge grin at her twin, Jessica grabbed the pen and signed her name in a dashing scrawl on the guest list. Ever since Jessica had met Jeremy Frank when she and Elizabeth were working as candy stripers at the local hospital, she had had an enormous crush on him. She had even managed once to wheedle her way into a guest appearance on "Frankly Speaking."

Elizabeth, Jeffrey, and Enid signed in, and the receptionist handed them each a red plastic visitor's badge. "Have a good time," she said, once she'd given them directions to the studio.

"We will," Jessica said airily, leading the way with a confident stride.

Enid kept her eyes fixed on Jessica's back. She had been to the station once before, and Richard's office was down this same corridor.

Suddenly a familiar voice called out. "Enid! What brings you here?"

She froze. This was exactly what she had been dreading. "Hi, Richard," she mumbled as she turned around to meet him.

"Well, I don't suppose you came to see me," he said. He gave the others a friendly smile, but he looked tired and withdrawn, and Enid heard an edge of sarcasm in his voice.

"These are my friends. You know Liz, and

this is her sister, Jessica, and Jeffrey French," Enid said, avoiding Richard's eyes. "This is Richard Cernak. He's the program director here," she added for Jessica and Jeffrey's benefit.

"Hi," Elizabeth said, politely extending her hand. She shot a puzzled glance at Enid and turned to Richard again. "We're here to interview Jeremy Frank for a documentary we're making about Sweet Valley."

Surprise registered on Richard's face. "You are? Enid never mentioned a word about it," he said. She looked down and said nothing.

"If she had," Richard continued, "I would have offered to get you access to our video equipment." He turned to Jeffrey and gave the video camera an appraising look. "That takes the same size tape as ours. I could arrange for you to use our editing machines if you'd like. That will give it a good, polished look."

"Can we really?" Jeffrey asked, his green eyes shining. He and Elizabeth exchanged eager glances, and he nodded quickly. "That would be fantastic, Mr. Cernak. We'd really appreciate it."

"No problem. Just give me a call when you're ready to put it all together, and I'll make the arrangements for you."

"Thank you so much, Mr. Cernak," Elizabeth said warmly.

"Call me Richard. My only condition is that I want to see this epic when it's done!"

Elizabeth shook his hand again. "It's a deal!"

As Richard headed toward his office, Enid clenched her jaw and started down the corridor again.

"What's wrong?" Elizabeth asked in an undertone, walking alongside her as Jessica and Jeffrey rushed ahead.

Enid shrugged but didn't say anything.

"I thought you were acting sort of weird with Richard." Elizabeth went on awkwardly. "Don't you usually get along with him?"

"I just don't really like him very much."

"Oh." Elizabeth was silent for a moment, then added, "Anyway, he said we could use all the editing equipment. Isn't that great?"

Enid stopped and put her hand on Elizabeth's arm. "He's only doing it to try to get me to like him, you know," she said tersely.

A disappointed look flickered in Elizabeth's eyes. "But, Enid, what's wrong with that? It doesn't make his offer any less generous, does it?"

"I don't know," she replied. "All I know is he's making trouble at my house."

But in the back of her mind, Enid knew that it wasn't really Richard who was making the trouble. There hadn't been any trouble with him until her grandmother arrived. But she pushed that thought away and started walking again.

Enid knew that she must seem immature and selfish to Elizabeth. And that hurt, because Elizabeth's friendship meant everything to her. It was just too difficult to explain, and besides, even if she could explain, it wouldn't make any difference.

"Here's the studio," Elizabeth said softly.

Enid nodded and darted a quick look at her best friend. "I'm just being a jerk, Liz. Don't pay any attention to me, OK? OK?" she repeated with a cajoling smile.

"OK," Elizabeth agreed, returning her smile. "Now let's go and see Mr. Hunk. That is, if we can get a word in edgewise with Jessica around."

Nine

Enid looked up from her breakfast as her grandmother came into the kitchen.

"How did you sleep last night, Mother?" Mrs. Rollins asked, pouring coffee.

The elder woman smiled placidly. "Not too badly, for once, although the traffic going by woke me several times." Mrs. Langevin lowered herself into a chair at the table and added casually, "I suppose your bedroom is much quieter, Adele, being at the back of the house."

Looking up, Enid noticed her mother's mouth tighten into a stern, uncompromising line. She felt her stomach clench for a moment as she realized her mother wasn't going to say anything.

"Maybe Nana could have your room, Mom," she suggested finally.

"Oh, I don't want to put your mother out of her bedroom," Mrs. Langevin said. "I don't want to be a bother. But how sweet of you, dear."

Enid smiled faintly.

"Adele, this orange juice . . ."

"Yes, Mother? Is something wrong with it?"

Shrugging, Mrs. Langevin said, "It has so much pulp in it, dear. I find it difficult to digest."

Mrs. Rollins set her coffee cup down with a clunk. "Mother," she replied, her voice firmly controlled, "I squeezed that juice from oranges from the tree out back. I thought you might find it a treat after drinking frozen for so long."

"Of course, dear."

"Mom," Enid put in quickly. Her mother directed a fierce, warning glance at her, but she went on anyway. "It wouldn't be a big deal to strain it, would it?"

"Strain it yourself then, Enid," Mrs. Rollins snapped. She shook the newspaper open and buried her face in it.

Enid looked at her grandmother. She was calmly scraping butter off a piece of toast, apparently oblivious to their bickering.

"I was wondering," Mrs. Langevin said, still scraping away at her toast. "I'd like to pick up some things in town today."

"Just let me know what you'd like, Mother. I can get them for you on my way home."

"Oh. Adele, I thought it might be nice if I could go myself so I can compare prices. But of course you're busy. It doesn't matter at all what I want."

Mrs. Rollins lowered her newspaper with a sigh and stood up to clear her dishes from the table. "Of course it does, Mother. Don't say that. I suppose Enid can drive me to work, then take you after school."

"Mom—" Her heart thumping, Enid gave her mother a meaningful look. "I promised Liz I'd help her out with the documentary today, and I've already stood her up a few times." She nervously rubbed her palms together under the table. "Could I take you tomorrow, Nana?" Enid asked tentatively.

Her grandmother looked annoyed. "It's only a few things, but I wanted them today."

For a long moment, Enid stared at the sugar bowl in the center of the table. There had to be some way to get out of this. She didn't want to tell Elizabeth again she couldn't make the taping—not that Elizabeth ever minded or made any objections, but Enid just hated to disappoint her.

"I could pick them up on my way back if you tell me what you want and how much you wanted to spend, Nana," she said in a low voice. "Or we could go after dinner—the stores at the mall are open late. But I really can't cancel my plans with Liz. It wouldn't be fair."

"No, Enid. There's a program on after dinner I want to see. But really," her grandmother continued, sounding wounded, "if you'd rather spend your time having fun with your friends, I understand. I can see how your friends might be more important to you than I am."

"Of course not, Nana! That's not it at all," Enid said hastily, although she couldn't put very much feeling into it. A week ago she would have said she'd do anything for her grandmother, but now . . .

She swallowed hard. She didn't want to back down, but there didn't seem to be much choice. "We can go as soon as I get home from school." Maybe there would be time to catch up with Elizabeth and the others after they ran the errands.

Her grandmother beamed at her and reached across the table to pat her hand. "You're such a dear, and I do appreciate it so much. I'll be ready and waiting for you."

"Enid?"

"Y-yes, Mr. Collins?" Enid responded sheepishly.

"I said, what did you feel was the most important element in the story?"

A hot flush swept up Enid's face as she met Mr. Collins's eyes. He was smiling at her encouragingly, but she couldn't think of anything to say.

"I—well . . ."

"Mr. Collins?" Caroline Pearce raised her hand, and the handsome English teacher turned away from Enid with a shrug. She slumped down in her chair and let out a long breath. So far she had been totally distracted in every class that morning. She just couldn't concentrate on her work.

She looked dully out the window, her mind blank. Nothing seemed to be going right these days. And she couldn't understand why having her grandmother live with them should cause so much trouble. There was no question for Enid that it was Nana who was creating all the tension. Enid and her mother were constantly arguing about everything. It was as though Nana was a stranger, and since they didn't know how to act around *her*, that made them upset with each other.

And if that wasn't enough of a problem, things with Hugh kept going downhill. Even though they were planning to go to the Beach Disco on Friday night, Enid could tell he was still hurt about the canceled field trip. When they had talked on the phone the previous night, his voice had had a distant tone to it that was becoming painfully familiar. As worried as she was about their relationship, she couldn't think of any way to improve it. She just felt lost and alone.

The bell rang, and Enid escaped gratefully to the hall, grabbed her lunch from her locker, and went to the cafeteria. There she found Elizabeth and a group of their friends sitting at a large table. She pulled out a chair and sat down without a word.

Ken Matthews was recounting his victory at the county fair pie-eating contest the summer before. "I had already eaten one blueberry pie, and I could see Winston was halfway through his second. I wondered how anyone so thin could eat so fast."

"You're sure it wasn't his third?" Maria Santelli, Winston's girlfriend, said dryly. She poked Winston in the ribs, and he let out a shrill yelp.

"Skinny people always eat like hogs," Elizabeth said with a laugh. "Take Enid here—you should see what she does to a carton of ice cream."

Enid's face burned. "That's not very funny, Liz."

There was an embarrassed silence at the table, and Elizabeth's eyes widened with alarm. "I'm sorry, Enid. I didn't mean . . ."

They stared at each other for a long moment,

and before Enid realized what was happening, she burst into tears. Her friends looked awkwardly at one another, stunned into silence. With a strangled cry, she pushed herself to her feet and stumbled away.

"Oh, no," Elizabeth whispered. She turned to Jeffrey. "I never—I didn't—"

He took her hand. "I know you didn't mean anything. Something must really be bothering her."

Elizabeth shook her head. "I don't know what happened," she said, "but I'm going to find out right now."

Pushing her half-eaten lunch away, Elizabeth rose and hurried after Enid. Out in the hallway she saw her best friend entering the girls' lavatory.

She followed her inside "Enid?" she called softly.

Her friend's voice came from the last stall. "Yeah, I'm here."

"Enid, what's wrong?" Elizabeth asked. The door wasn't closed all the way. Enid was leaning against the metal wall of the stall. She sobbed softly, her face half buried in her arms.

Elizabeth's heart swelled with pity. "Won't you tell me what's been bugging you lately? I can see you're really upset about something, but you're keeping it all bottled up inside."

Enid's curls bobbed as she shook her head,

and she raised a trembling hand to wipe away the tears. "It's nothing, Liz. Really."

"Enid! Please! I just feel so bad for you. I wish you'd come out and tell me what's wrong."

Enid sniffed softly, opened the door all the way, and came out. The pain in her eyes went straight to Elizabeth's heart. "I don't know what to do, Liz," she said in a shaky voice. "I thought it would be so great to have Nana with us, but everything's gone wrong! I mean, I *want* to be with her, but when she makes it so I don't have any choice, I just get so angry!" She shook her head dejectedly and stared down at the floor.

"Can't you talk to her about it? Let her know that you have things to do on your own?" Elizabeth offered gently. "Or could your mother talk to her?"

Enid heaved a sigh of resignation. "I don't know. I can't really talk about it anymore, Liz. I don't even know myself what I'm thinking. But I'm sorry for acting like such a idiot."

"Forget about it. I just wanted you to know we're worried about you."

"Yeah, I know." Enid walked to the wall dispenser and pulled out a paper towel to wipe her nose. Then she looked in the mirror and fingered her hair. "I look like a lonely orphan."

With a sad smile, Elizabeth put one arm across Enid's shoulders and met her eyes in the mirror. "I know it'll work out, Enid. But you have to stick up for yourself a little more."

Enid laughed ruefully. "Yeah, that's me. I'm always such a wimp."

"I'm not even going to answer that one," Elizabeth retorted loyally. She gave Enid a warm squeeze. "Are you coming back to finish lunch?"

Enid shook her head and sniffled. "I think I'll just go to the library and read or something." She smiled bravely. "Go on, I'll be all right. People have to fall apart every once in a while. It's just my turn," she said lightly, dabbing again at her eyes.

With one last look, Elizabeth turned and walked to the door. "Enid—?"

Her friend nodded. "I'll be OK. Thanks, Liz."

Edgy with impatience, Enid jingled the car keys in her pocket and glanced up the stairs yet again. She could hear her grandmother walking to and fro above as she was getting ready to go out.

At last Mrs. Langevin started down the steps, her handbag clutched tightly in one hand. As she reached the bottom, she smiled at Enid.

"I'm sorry I wasn't ready, dear. I overslept my nap. Just like an old hibernating bear, I'm afraid." She patted Enid on the cheek and gave her a tiny wink.

Instantly, Enid's impatience evaporated. This was the Nana she remembered. She smiled back warmly. "That's OK, Nana. Are you ready now?"

"I certainly am. Let's go."

By the time they reached the drugstore in the mall, Enid's nerves were strained to the breaking point again. Her grandmother had managed to find something to complain about almost every minute of the ride. The sun's glare was too strong, or she didn't like the radio station Enid picked, or they were parked too far from the mall entrance. Enid bore with it for her grandmother's sake, but it was getting harder by the minute.

Now she watched as Mrs. Langevin pored over the selection of aspirin and other pain relievers in the big drugstore. "Things are certainly more expensive here than in my old neighborhood," she said. She picked up a bottle of capsules, looked at the price, and shook her head.

"Mom always takes those for a headache," Enid put in quickly. She stole a peek at her watch and groaned inwardly. "She thinks they work very well."

"Well, it seems to me I bought that brand once before and the cap was so difficult to get off I had to throw the whole bottle away."

Enid restrained a sigh and pointed farther

along the shelf. "Nana, here's one that comes in a nonchildproof container. It's very easy to open."

"Hmm." Mrs. Langevin wrinkled her nose as she peered at the price on the label. "And more expensive than the others, too. No, not that one," she decided, putting it back after long consideration. "Where are the buffered aspirin? My stomach acts up terribly if I don't take a buffered aspirin."

"Nana, we have aspirin at home, too, you know. Buffered aspirin. There's no reason why you shouldn't use it."

With a wave of her hand, her grandmother dismissed the offer. "No, Enid. I intend to provide for myself as much as I can. I don't want to be a bother to you or your mother."

Enid nearly cried with frustration. It seemed as though every time her grandmother insisted she didn't want to be a bother, she was being the most difficult to get along with! And no matter how hard Enid tried to be accommodating and helpful, her grandmother had something to complain about. Nothing was quite right; nothing was acceptable the way it was.

It occurred to Enid that although she and her mother were bending over backward to be nice, her grandmother wasn't even trying to meet them halfway. She was picky, demanding, crotchety . . .

A fierce wave of shame washed over Enid. True, her grandmother was definitely being difficult, but she was widowed, in a strange new place, with no friends of her own—and her own granddaughter was acting like a selfish, spoiled brat because she had to drive her downtown on errands.

"I'll just be a moment, dear," her grandmother said, as though reading her thoughts. "Then I'd like to look for some hairspray."

Enid nodded faintly, blinking back tears. At this rate they wouldn't be home until dinnertime. But it hardly seemed to matter anymore. She wasn't part of Elizabeth's documentary at this point, and she'd just have to accept it. There was nothing else she could do.

Ten

Guy Chesney, keyboardist for the Droids, played a few experimental chords and made some adjustments to the row of knobs on his equalizer. The rest of the band, Dan Scott, Emily Mayer, Dana Larson, and Max Dellon, fiddled with equipment and microphones as the Beach Disco hummed with excited voices. Sweet Valley's hottest student rock band always played to a packed house.

"Do you want something to drink?" Hugh asked Enid above the sound of the crowd.

She met his eyes, trying to read what was behind them. But they told her nothing. She nodded. As Hugh stood up and began weaving his way through the crowd, she felt her heart turn over painfully. This evening *had* to be good. They *had* to get things back on track.

"Enid! Hi." Her eyes brilliant with excitement, Elizabeth sat down next to Enid. "You look so pretty tonight," she went on. "That's a good color for you."

"Thanks," Enid said shyly. "I'm giving it everything I've got tonight," she confessed, glancing down at her green halter-dress and white sandals.

Elizabeth lowered her voice. "Are things going a little better with you and Hugh?"

"Well . . . if all goes well tonight." She looked around. "Where's Jeffrey?"

"Setting up the camera. Back there." Elizabeth nodded toward the back of the dance floor. Craning her neck, Enid could just make him out, surrounded by Sweet Valley students.

"Is Jessica doing more interviews tonight?"

"Yes. Oh, by the way," Elizabeth added, turning quickly back to Enid and putting her hand on her knee. "After tonight, we'll be about finished. Do you think you could arrange with Richard for us to do the editing next week?"

With a small nod, Enid agreed, and Hugh returned with two cups of soda.

Just then, the Droids played their opening chord, and an expectant hush fell over the room. Enid turned to face the stage. Dana stepped forward to her microphone and gave the crowd a cool, appraising glance.

"I hope you all realize this is a momentous occasion," she began, shifting from one foot to the other. She gestured to the back of the room where Jeffrey was taping the crowd. "Tonight we're on film, Sweet Valley. So let's make this a *hot night.*"

There was a round of enthusiastic applause and cheering, and Dana grinned. "We're going to start out with a little tune I think some of you might know," she said. "One, two, one, two, three, four!"

The Droids launched into "Meltdown," one of their most popular songs. Within seconds, people all over the disco were up and dancing.

"Come on," said Hugh, standing up and holding out his hand to Enid. He gave her a tender smile.

Relief swept through her, and she sent Elizabeth a smile as she stood up to join him. Elizabeth gave her the thumbs-up sign. *Let everything be all right,* Enid prayed fervently as Hugh took her in his arms. *Please let everything work out.*

"What would you say is the best thing about living in Sweet Valley?" Jessica prompted.

Bruce Patman tossed his thick black hair out of his eyes and gave the camera an arrogant smile. "Well, speaking as a member of Sweet Valley's founding family, I'd have to say that its people are the best in the state," he said smoothly.

While the camera was on Bruce, Jessica took the opportunity to stick her tongue out at him and cross her eyes, trying to make him lose his cool composure. It always riled her when he pulled that "founding family" business. Just because he was rich and handsome and drove his own Porsche didn't mean he would survive the editing, she told herself with satisfaction. She hoped he would end up on the cutting-room floor.

There was a big crowd clustered around Jessica and Jeffrey out on the deck, all eager to take their turns in front of the camera.

"Hey, Jess, when is this movie going to be done?" Neil Fremount, a member of the Sweet Valley High tennis team, asked.

She turned to her twin, her eyebrows lifted in a question.

"It'll be finished by next weekend, we hope," Elizabeth said. "We'll be doing the editing during the week."

Cara Walker was sitting on the railing beside Penny and Neil. "Hey, you should have a premiere—like they do with the big Hollywood movies."

Jessica stared at her friend. "Cara! That is an

amazing idea! Liz," she exclaimed, whirling around to her twin, "can we be ready by next Saturday night? Say yes!"

"Yes!" Elizabeth said with a laugh.

"Then it's all set. First showing, our house, Saturday night. What a great idea! Cara, you're a genius."

A short distance away, Enid glanced up at Hugh's profile and slipped her hand through his arm. "You'll come, won't you—to the premiere?" she asked hopefully. Even though he had spent a lot of time with her friends, she knew he still felt like an outsider with them sometimes.

He nodded. "Sure. It sounds like fun."

"It will be," she said hugging his arm to her side. "It will be."

Later, at home, Elizabeth sat on her bed as Jessica chattered away at her from the bathroom. "Now don't forget, we're expecting you and Jeffrey to come to cheerleading practice on Tuesday to get us in action. Don't forget."

"I won't, Jess."

"And I promised Lila that in return for borrowing her camera all this time, we'd make sure to put in her interview."

Elizabeth sighed and stood up to unzip her

dress. "OK, Jess, fair enough. Whatever you say."

"Also"—Jessica poked her head through the bathroom doorway, her face covered in cold cream—"I have cheerleading practice on Thursday, so I can't go to the TV station. You'll have to do the editing without me." She disappeared again into the bathroom.

Shaking her head, Elizabeth hung up her dress. It was typical of her twin: stay for the fun and leave when the real work got started. But she had never expected Jessica to stick with the project this long anyway, so she didn't mind.

What she did mind, though, was the nagging suspicion that Enid wouldn't be able to help out, either. Enid had insisted that she would definitely try to make it, but by now Elizabeth knew she couldn't count on her. It didn't have anything to do with Enid's reliability, It had everything to do with the way Enid's life was being taken over.

Elizabeth sighed wearily. She knew Enid was too softhearted to say no to someone she loved. And Elizabeth thought she had a pretty good idea of what was happening over at the Rollins house. Every time her grandmother wanted something, Enid was undoubtedly rushing off to provide it as fast as she could. Elizabeth guessed that the day she and Jeffrey and Jessica were at Enid's house was typical of the way things were going. Elizabeth knew that people who were kind and generous were often taken advantage of. And it must be even worse because Enid had been expecting her grandmother to be a friend, not a burden.

Saddened by her thought, Elizabeth sank down onto her bed and reached for a notepad. There were some last-minute scenes to shoot before the editing on Thursday. If they had the time, she wanted to get up to Secca Lake, a popular picnic area, and she also wanted to try videotaping from the open convertible while driving through downtown Sweet Valley. She and Jeffrey could do that without Jessica. What worried her was that they would probably have to do it without Enid, too.

Eleven

The next week on Thursday afternoon Elizabeth and Jeffrey returned to the television station, their precious videotapes stashed in her straw bag.

"I can't believe we're actually doing this," Elizabeth said as they stepped inside the lobby.

"I know. Me, neither. But we are."

Elizabeth spoke to the receptionist. "Hi. I'm Elizabeth Wakefield, and this is Jeffrey French. We have an appointment with Mr. Cernak."

The receptionist nodded and swung her hair back as she put the phone to her ear. "Mr. Cernak will be right out," she said a minute later.

Elizabeth looked around the lobby, taking in the rows of comfortable chairs and autographed photographs of celebrities on the walls. It was a thrilling atmosphere.

"Liz! Jeffrey! How are you?" Richard Cernak rounded the corner into the lobby, hands outstretched in welcome. A puzzled expression crossed his face as he added, "Where's Enid?"

"She had to stay at home with her grandmother," Elizabeth explained, feeling a fresh twinge of disappointment. It hadn't been much of a surprise when Enid told them she couldn't make it to the station. But it had hurt just the same.

Richard Cernak shook his head sadly and looked as though he might comment. Instead, he shrugged and nodded back toward the studios. "Come on. I'll take you to the editing rooms and get you set up. I've also asked one of our editors, Emma Gold, to help you out if you need it. She'll be here all afternoon."

As he talked, he led the way down the hallway. Soon they arrived at a room with a sign, Editing, on the door.

"Here we are," he said, opening the door and ushering them inside. "Emma, here are some friends of mine to put together a documentary about Sweet Valley. Liz and Jeffrey."

A petite, dark-haired woman turned around in her swivel chair. "Hi." She was seated in front of a row of videotape editing machines, and scattered around her were pages of notes and reference books.

"OK. I don't suppose either one of you has used one of these before, right?" Richard said, advancing toward the video editors. Elizabeth and Jeffrey shook their heads.

"I suggest that you start by running through all your tape, to remind yourself of what you've got. Then you'll begin to have ideas on how to put it all together."

Elizabeth walked forward eagerly. "I wrote down the order I'd like things to go in," she said. She looked at the controls and screens and threw a smile over her shoulder at Jeffrey.

"Is this the first?" Richard said as he opened a box. Elizabeth nodded. "OK. It goes in here. Here's the Play button, and the Fast Forward and Rewind. Now just watch, and let the ideas come to you. I'll be in my office if you need me."

"Thank you so much, Richard," Jeffrey said as he joined Elizabeth at the console. They watched as he left the room and then turned their attention to the video screen in front of them.

"The hardest part will be cutting it down to an hour," Elizabeth observed as Jessica appeared on the monitor. "Doesn't she look great? I have a feeling we're going to want to keep everything."

"Yeah, but let's start."

"Ohhh." Elizabeth squeezed her eyes shut and let out a groan of utter fatigue. "Six hours. We've spent six hours on this, can you believe it?"

Jeffrey arched his back and rolled his shoulders around a couple of times. "No," he admitted. "It feels like we just went through a sudden-death playoff in the Super Bowl. But I think we're finished, aren't we?"

"Mmm." Rubbing her eyes again, Elizabeth turned back to the glowing screen they had been hunched over all afternoon. "Think we should go through it one more time?" she asked.

With an emphatic shake of his head, Jeffrey stood up and held out his hand to her. "No. It's perfect now."

"You really think so?" she asked as she put her hand in his and stood up. She looked at the one cassette that held their edited tape. It seemed a miracle that they could have condensed two weeks of taping into a one-hour documentary. But they had! And Elizabeth knew it would make a good addition to the video showcase. She could hardly wait to see everyone's reaction at their premiere Saturday night.

"How about getting something to eat on the way home?" Jeffrey asked.

"Good idea. Let's go."

They collected their tapes and notes, said good-bye to Emma Gold, and slipped out the door into the quiet hallway.

Up ahead, around the corner, they could hear voices. As they walked forward, the voices grew louder; they sounded strained and tense. Elizabeth and Jeffrey looked at each other silently.

Then Elizabeth stopped and pulled Jeffrey back. At the same moment he paused, too, and they exchanged another worried look. It was Richard Cernak and Mrs. Rollins who were arguing.

"What should we do?" Elizabeth whispered.

"Richard, I can't leave Mother by herself again this Saturday," they heard Mrs. Rollins say. "It just isn't fair to her."

"I understand your point, Adele. I really do. But this broadcasters' dinner Saturday night is a once-a-year event. I don't really want to go either, but I'm obligated to. Don't you see—"

"I *do* see. Of course I do. I know it's important for your career, Richard." Mrs. Rollins sighed heavily. She sounded very tired. "But think how my mother must feel. Ever since she moved in, I've been out three or four times a week in the evenings, and poor Enid's social life is suffering because of it. She doesn't want to leave Mother alone when I'm gone."

There was a long pause. Elizabeth winced in embarrassment. It would be too mortifying for everyone if the adults knew their conversation was being overheard. All she could hope was that the argument would be over soon and that Mrs. Rollins and Richard would go away.

"Adele. Just this one more time. Please."

"Oh, all right," Mrs. Rollins agreed wearily. "But after that, I really have to put in some time with Mother."

"I know, sweetheart. Thank you so much."

Footsteps receded down the corridor, and Elizabeth and Jeffrey heaved sighs of relief. "Boy, I'm glad that's over," Elizabeth muttered.

"Me, too." Jeffrey squeezed her hand for reassurance as they headed around the corner. He looked down at her. "You don't think this will mean Enid can't come to the party on Saturday, do you?"

Elizabeth considered. "I hope not. I don't think so. It's not as if her grandmother were an invalid. For something special like this, I'm sure Mrs. Langevin wouldn't mind staying home alone for one night."

"You're probably right," Jeffrey said. "This Saturday night *is* going to be special. I know Enid wouldn't miss it."

Enid put away the leftovers from dinner, shut the refrigerator door, and wearily leaned her forehead against it. But a visual impression stayed with her. She opened the door again and reached for a jar of applesauce. That was just the sort of thing she wanted.

She sat down at the table and began eating applesauce out of the jar with a spoon, just as she used to do when she was little. For some reason, it was comforting. She smiled to herself, and then heard a car door slam outside.

"Hi, Enid," her mother said a moment later as she let herself in the back door. "Mmm. Applesauce. I could go for some of that myself, right now."

Enid smiled up at her mother, glad that the tension they had been feeling lately was gone for the moment. "Want to share my spoon?" she offered.

"You bet." Mrs. Rollins sat down across from her and held out her hands for the jar and spoon.

"Where's Nana?" she asked.

"In the living room watching TV."

"No, I'm not!" With a little chuckle, Mrs. Langevin poked her head through the kitchen doorway. "I thought I heard you come in, Adele. Had a good day?"

"Hi, Mother. Not bad. Here, have a seat." Mrs. Rollins pulled out a chair.

Enid felt a lump rise in her throat as the three of them sat there together. This was the way it should be all the time, she told herself. Comfortable, friendly, and happy.

Her grandmother folded her hands on the table and looked at Mrs. Rollins with an expectant smile. "Well, you'll be happy to hear I finally took a look at that schedule for the senior center, Adele."

"Did you? That's great, Mother. Did you see anything that looks interesting?"

"I did. They're showing a special movie I've heard about. It didn't get a big release when it first came out," Mrs. Langevin explained. "But the senior center has it for one showing this month."

Setting down the applesauce jar, Mrs. Rollins let out a contented sigh. "That sounds wonderful, Mother. I'd be happy to take you. When is it?"

"That would be lovely. It's on Saturday night."

Instantly Mrs. Rollins's peaceful smile faded. "Oh, Mother. I'm sorry. Saturday is the *one* night I can't. I have to go to an awards dinner with Richard."

Enid felt her heart begin pounding furiously. *Not again!* she cried to herself. She knew what was coming, and she gritted her teeth in anticipation.

"Oh. I understand," Mrs. Langevin said in a small voice.

"Maybe Enid could take you," Mrs. Rollins

said in a hopeful tone as she looked at her daughter.

Enid pressed her lips together and stared hard to the tablecloth. "Mom, that's the night of the premiere of Elizabeth's documentary. The twins are having a party, and Hugh's coming. It's really important to me. . . ." She looked up to meet her mother's eyes. *Please,* she begged silently. *Please say I can go! Don't let me down this time!*

Mrs. Rollins regarded her in silence for a long moment. An echo of the warmth and love and trust they had shared five minutes earlier was still with them. She nodded and gave Enid a small smile, then turned to her mother.

"I forgot about that party, Mother. I know it means a lot to Enid, and she's been staying at home so much lately."

A pained expression came into Mrs. Langevin's eyes, and she jutted out her chin obstinately. Enid's heart lurched, and a tense silence descended on the table as the two younger women waited for Enid's grandmother to say she didn't mind.

"The senior center always repeats its movies," Mrs. Rollins said with growing impatience. "I'm sure they'll have it again before long. But this time I think we ought to let Enid do what she wants."

Enid felt tears spring to her eyes as she waited.

She was go grateful and relieved that her mother was on her side again, finally. But there was a new, fresher pain in her heart because of the way her grandmother was acting.

"All right," Mrs. Langevin said at last, her eyes fixed on the far wall. "I understand." She pushed herself to her feet. "I think I'll go to bed now. I'm not feeling very well."

For a moment Enid was tempted to call her back and agree to go to the movie. But she caught a warning look from her mother and kept quiet. They waited until the door shut.

"Enid," her mother said quietly, putting one hand on her daughter's shoulder. "I think Nana is feeling a little sorry for herself, but I meant what I said. I think it's your turn to get what you want."

"I know, Mom, and I appreciate it, but . . ."

Standing up, Mrs. Rollins smoothed Enid's hair back from her forehead and kissed her softly. "I know you love her, Enid, and you're worried that you've hurt her. But you have your own life to live, just as I do, and just as Nana does. You've already been very generous about staying with her, and you deserve to have a little fun."

"But Nana looked so upset!"

"She'll get over it. I think she was just sort of surprised at not getting her way for the first time, that's all," Mrs. Rollins said, squeezing Enid's shoulder reassuringly.

Enid swallowed hard and put her hand up over her mother's. She didn't know if she was happy about going to the party after all or upset at letting her grandmother down or angry that it had been such a narrow victory. All she knew was that she was confused, and a little hurt, too.

"OK, Mom," she whispered, fighting back tears. "Thanks."

Twelve

"I just don't think it's fair," Jessica grumbled. She dumped a handful of blueberries into her cereal. "I made it, too, and I should get to see it."

Ned Wakefield, the twins' father, put down his newspaper and looked at Elizabeth. "Can we settle this out of court?" he teased, a sparkle in his eyes.

"There's nothing to settle," Elizabeth tossed back, consciously avoiding her sister's steely glare. "The premiere is tonight at eight, Jess. If you had come to help edit, you would have seen it already. But as it is . . ." She ducked her head behind the cereal boxes to hide her smile.

With an indignant snort, Jessica pushed her chair back and stood up with her bowl of cereal. "I don't have to stay here and take this abuse," she announced in a dignified tone. "I'm leaving."

"Liz, you're one tough customer," Mrs. Wakefield observed dryly as Jessica stormed out of the kitchen. "I expected you would have given in by now."

Elizabeth giggled. "I know. That's why Jeffrey has the tape at his house. I couldn't have kept it safe for so long under a prolonged Jessica attack."

"By the way, Liz, Steven called to say he'll be coming home from college to watch, too." Mrs. Wakefield reached for the coffeepot. "He said he wouldn't miss it for anything."

"We'll all be pretty anxious to see it by tonight, Liz," her father said with a smile. "So save us some aisle seats, huh?"

Enid paused outside her grandmother's room and knocked timidly. "Nana? Are you awake?" She pushed open the door, and froze.

Her grandmother was still in bed, staring at the ceiling. "Nana, aren't you getting up this morning?" she asked anxiously.

"I don't feel very well, Enid. I'm going to rest for a while longer."

Enid nodded and turned away, shutting the door behind her. Was Nana pretending, or was she really sick? Judging from what her mother had told her, it seemed more than likely that Mrs. Langevin just wanted sympathy and was angry because she was missing the movie at the senior center.

"I hope I'm right," Enid muttered as she trotted downstairs. She felt a pang of compassion but stubbornly brushed it aside. She was going to go to the party that night.

Her mother met her at the bottom of the steps. "Nana says she doesn't feel well," Enid told her. "She's staying in bed."

"Honestly," Mrs. Rollins said in exasperation, "she's acting like a spoiled child. Oh, well, don't worry about it, honey. I'm sure it's just an act."

"But still, Mom, I feel bad about leaving her alone tonight," Enid said as they walked into the living room. "Even if she isn't sick, she must be feeling kind of upset."

"I know. I called Mrs. Cutler, and she said she'd be glad to come over and stay with Nana this evening."

Enid breathed a sigh of relief. Mrs. Cutler was their next-door neighbor, and very friendly. "That's a good idea, Mom. Mrs. Cutler is really nice."

"Well, let's just hope Nana thinks so," her mother said gloomily, straightening the magazines on the coffee table. Their eyes met, and a ripple of apprehension passed between them.

"It's going to work out fine," Mrs. Rollins said emphatically. "Just fine."

"Enid, zip me up, would you?" Mrs. Rollins hurried into Enid's bedroom. She was wearing an elegant black cocktail dress and turned her back to her daughter.

"You look great, Mom."

Mrs. Rollins looked around, her eyes sparkling with excitement. "So do you, honey. I'm so glad you're going to Liz's party. I want to hear all about it later."

Nodding, Enid turned to her own mirror and ran her comb through her hair again. She needed to go to the party and have a good time. The tension at home had been growing worse all day, and she couldn't wait to escape. In spite of their attempts to cajole her grandmother into a good mood, she had remained sullen and cross since she got out of bed.

With a final glance in the mirror, Enid followed her mother downstairs.

"Richard will be here any minute," Mrs. Rollins was saying, clipping on a pair of onyx-and-silver earrings. "And Mrs. Cutler should be here pretty soon, too."

"OK, Mom. Hugh's picking me up at seven-thirty."

"Great—oh, and Enid? Be sure to write down the Wakefields' phone number."

Enid nodded, lost in thought. She couldn't shake the feeling that something was going to go wrong.

"Nana? I'm putting the phone number at Liz's house here by the phone," she said over her shoulder. She looked through the doorway into the living room. Her grandmother was sitting on the couch, arms folded across her chest.

"Is something wrong, Nana?" she asked tentatively. It was clear something was wrong, and she knew what it was. But she didn't want to seem uncaring.

"I've decided I don't want that woman to come here."

Enid stopped, stunned. "What?"

Mrs. Langevin nodded emphatically. "I said, I don't want some stranger coming here to stay with me. I don't like strangers, and I don't want to stay here alone with one."

"Mother!" Seething with exasperation, Mrs. Rollins came into the living room, her coat over her arm. "Why wait until the last minute to tell me this? Mrs. Cutler is a lovely woman. You'll like her. I *promise*."

"No," Mrs. Langevin said.

Enid knew disaster was about to strike.

Outside, a car horn began honking, and Mrs. Rollins looked quickly out the window. "Mother!"

"I don't want her here, and that's final."

Mrs. Rollins clenched her jaw and strode angrily to the telephone. "Fine. If that's the way you want it, that's the way you'll have it." She punched the numbers on the telephone, tapping her foot with impatience as she waited for the phone on the other end to be picked up. "Denise? I'm so glad I caught you. It's Adele . . . No, I hate to do this to you, but Mother says she'd rather be alone . . . No . . . I know, Denise. I'm very sorry to put you to any inconvenience. Thanks. Bye."

She hung up the phone with a clatter and cast another exasperated look at the front door as she returned to the living room for her coat and evening bag. "There. Satisfied?" she shouted at her mother.

Mrs. Langevin pressed her lips together and put one hand on her heart. "You'll have to stay home, now, Adele. I can't be here alone. I might get sick."

"What?"

The door bell rang, and Richard's voice came through the door. "Adele? Are you ready?" Enid's eyes widened in alarm.

Mrs. Rollins furiously pushed her arms into the sleeves of her coat and looked at Enid. "I'm sorry, Enid. This is the last time." She turned and headed for the front door.

"No!" Outraged, Enid rushed after her. "Mom, wait! You can't—" The door slammed.

"Enid?" Her grandmother's voice reached her

from the living room. "Enid, I think I need my medicine."

Choking with tears, Enid stared at the front door. *This can't be happening!* she thought wildly.

"Enid?"

Enid was trembling with anger and disappointment as she turned to go back into the living room. Her grandmother looked up from her magazine with a faint smile. "Enid, will you please get me my medicine? I left it upstairs."

Enid stared at her in disbelief. Her grandmother had just ruined her evening, and she was smiling? "Nana—" She broke off as the door bell rang, and her heart turned over with a sickening lurch. It was Hugh.

With feet as heavy as lead, she retraced her steps to the front door and opened it slowly, dreading the inevitable confrontation. Before Hugh could speak, she said bluntly, "I can't go."

For a moment he regarded her without speaking. The bouquet of flowers he was holding fell to his side. Enid could see his jaw tightening.

"My grandmother says she's sick. My mother is gone. I can't leave her here by herself."

"I can't believe you're doing this to me," Hugh said finally, with growing anger. "Do you think this is funny or something? Is that it? It's some kind of a kick, standing me up all the time?"

131

Too tired and upset to argue, Enid leaned her forehead against the door and muttered. "Just go without me, Hugh. There's no reason you have to miss the party, too."

"Are you kidding? I'm not going without you. They're your friends, not mine. Remember?"

"What is that supposed to mean?" Enid demanded, growing angry herself. "You know Liz. You know Jeffrey. You've been out with them both.

"Listen," Hugh said, "just forget it. Give me a call sometime when you've got a few free minutes. Maybe I'll be around." With that he turned and strode to his car, leaving Enid dazed.

Tires squealing, the car pulled away and raced down the street. Tears streaming down her cheeks, Enid watched until it was out of sight. At the edge of the light from the open door, she could see the scattered flowers. With a choking sob, she stumbled down the steps and picked them up.

"Hugh!" It was a pitiful, mournful cry of despair. She was sure their relationship was over for good. She would never see him again. In anguish, she went back into the house, closed the door, and headed for the stairs.

"Enid?"

For a moment, Enid couldn't see a thing, she was so furious. She stopped in the living room doorway and stared at her grandmother. "What?" she said in a low, quavering voice.

Her grandmother raised her eyebrows inquis-itively. "Sounds like you and Hugh were having a fight."

"Yes. I think we probably just broke up, but I'm not sure," Enid answered painfully, fight-ing tears.

"Well, I'm sure it was for the best," Mrs. Langevin said calmly. "He wasn't worth it."

Enid felt her eyes widen, and suddenly some-thing snapped.

"How can you say that?" she cried, her hands clenched around the flowers. "I love Hugh, and you've ruined it! You've ruined everything, Nana! I hate you! I wish you'd never come here!" she cried. "Why don't you just leave?"

Time seemed to stop. To Enid, it felt as if the only two people on earth were her and her grandmother, staring at each other in grief, shock, and disbelief. Mrs. Langevin drew her-self up stiffly and threw her head back in defiance.

"Fine. If that's the way you want it, go ahead and leave me here all by myself! Go ahead and have fun with your friends. I'm sure they need your company more than I do," she said bit-terly. "I'm just a poor old woman!"

Enid thought her heart would break, but she wouldn't give in. "No, you're not! You just think you are. I don't know why you can't stay home by yourself! It wouldn't matter that much, would it?"

"I never thought you could be so selfish, Enid."

"Selfish! What do you think I've been doing ever since you got here?" she shouted as tears streamed down her cheeks. "I've been staying home and missing dates and breaking promises to my friends." She stopped on a gasp, throwing a desperate look at the front door. Turning back, sobbing, she added, "And you haven't once offered to let me go out instead of staying with you. Not once!"

Her grandmother remained silent. Spots of color began to burn on her cheeks.

"Go ahead, Nana," Enid sobbed, her fists clenched at her sides. "Go ahead and tell me I can go out! Tell me you don't mind! Tell me you understand I have a life, too!"

For her answer, Mrs. Langevin stalked past Enid and climbed the stairs. Still sobbing, Enid threw the flowers to the floor and grabbed the keys to her mother's car. Then she ran out of the house and slammed the door.

Thirteen

Jessica twirled around in front of her mirror and threw a brilliant smile over her shoulder at Cara.

"Well? How do I look? Like a star?"

Cara, who was sitting on the bed, gave her friend a nonchalant shrug. "Mmm. Yes, I guess I'd definitely have to say star material there, Jess."

"Great. I can't wait,"' Jessica crowed and swooped across the room to her dresser to select a scarf. After throwing half a dozen to the floor, Jessica finally chose a bright blue one spangled with gold and draped it around her throat.

"Hey," she said as she turned around again. "You're looking sort of upset, Cara. What's wrong?"

"Nothing," Cara replied hastily. She smiled. "So when's Steven getting here?" Steven Wakefield, the twins' eighteen-year-old brother, was a freshman at a college not far from Sweet Valley and often came home on weekends to see his family and Cara, whom he'd been dating for a while.

Jessica eyed herself in the mirror again, adjusting her scarf and sneaking a look at Cara's reflection.

"He got here about five. But he had this great idea to rent a giant screen projection TV. So he and Dad went out to get it."

Cara nodded thoughtfully, a faraway look in her eyes.

"Hey, is something wrong between you and Steve?" Jessica demanded.

"No," Cara said, too quickly. She shrugged and pushed herself up from the bed. "People will be getting here any minute, Jess. Don't you think we should go down?"

For a moment, Jessica regarded her friend solemnly. Something was definitely on Cara's mind, and it would require further investigation.

But for the time being, she was going to put it aside. All the excitement of the premiere came sweeping back over Jessica. This was *her* night, and she wasn't going to let anything distract her from it.

                    *   *   *

Elizabeth hurried to open the door. On the
front steps were Aaron Dallas, Jeffrey's best
friend, and his girlfriend, Heather Sanford.
Coming up the walk right behind them were Bill
Chase and DeeDee Gordon.

"Hi, everyone! Come on in," Elizabeth exclaimed. "The show starts in ten minutes!"

Nearly all the guests had arrived, but there
still wasn't a sign of Enid. *Where can she be?*
Elizabeth wondered.

She shut the door and met Jeffrey's eyes across
the room. He was standing with her brother,
admiring the huge projection television. He
shrugged slightly.

Turning away, Elizabeth checked for the last
time to see if everything was ready. The family
had transformed the living room into a minia-
ture theater: there were rows of chairs, and bowls
filled with buttered popcorn on every table. On
the walls were the posters Jessica had been
working on all afternoon: "World Premiere" and
"Exclusive First Night Showing" they announced
in bright letters. The atmosphere was charged
with anticipation. It would be perfect, Elizabeth
thought, if she could just set her mind at ease
about Enid.

"Liz, this was such a great idea," an excited
voice said at her elbow.

Startled from her reverie, Elizabeth faced

Lynne Henry, an attractive, shy girl who wrote songs for The Droids. With a big smile, Elizabeth nodded, but her thoughts remained on Enid. Lynne moved off with her boyfriend Guy Chesney, to find seats. Across the room Elizabeth could see her twin perched on the couch, surrounded by a crowd of friends. Jessica was clearly taking advantage of her new celebrity status, and the documentary hadn't even been shown yet!

Elizabeth glanced at her watch and hurried to the kitchen. She was about to pick up the telephone and dial Enid's number when her sister leaned around the half-open door. "Liz!" she called. "Come on, let's start!"

"But Enid isn't here yet," Elizabeth said.

Jessica rolled her eyes and glanced over her shoulder impatiently. "I can't— Oh, hang on a second, Liz. She just came in. Now we can start!"

Relief swept over Elizabeth, and she followed her twin back to the living room, where everyone had taken seats. She caught a glimpse of Enid slipping into a chair by the far wall. Elizabeth noticed that her face was pale and that she was alone.

But before Elizabeth could walk over to find out what was wrong, Jessica hopped up onto a chair and yelled for quiet.

"OK, everybody, this is it! Liz, get up here!

The director, everyone!" Jessica jumped down off the chair.

With a last worried glance at Enid, Elizabeth made her way to the front of the room to a round of applause.

"Speech! Speech!" her friends chanted.

Laughing, Elizabeth put one arm across Jessica's shoulder and one across Jeffrey's. She motioned to Enid to join them, but Enid shook her head emphatically.

"OK. Thank you all for coming," she said. "All I really want to say is that I hope you enjoy our video, and Jessica will be signing autographs later."

There was a burst of applause and laughter, and Jessica punched Elizabeth's arm playfully. Mr. Wakefield shut off the lights, and Steven pressed the Play button on the VCR as the room grew quiet. Elizabeth, Jessica, and Jeffrey sat down together in front, holding hands in nervous anticipation.

Instantly the huge screen lit up, and Jessica appeared, almost life-size. There was applause from the audience as her voice announced, "Welcome to Sweet Valley, California. My hometown!"

Then a series of images replaced her: pounding ocean waves, gulls circling above the beach, and the palm trees lining the road out to the mall. One by one, the faces of students of Sweet

Valley High flashed onto the screen: Neil Freemount hitting a tennis ball; the cheerleaders forming a pyramid; Winston Egbert, Tom McKay, Ken Matthews, and Aaron Dallas pressing their noses flat against the cafeteria window; Olivia Davidson, Penny Ayala, and Mr. Collins in the newspaper office; Lila Fowler in her lime-green Triumph. Face after face flickered across the screen, and each one was greeted with screams of laughter and thunderous applause.

Then Jessica was back, explaining the early history of the town. Elizabeth felt herself grinning as she waited for Winston to appear with the arrow through his head. When he did, the entire crowd roared with laughter, and Jessica shrieked in protest.

"I could kill you for leaving that in!" she cried.

"Hey, Win, how did you get that arrow taken out?" Ken Matthews called out in the darkness, and was immediately hushed by the audience.

Then a moving shot of downtown Sweet Valley appeared on the screen. Familiar storefronts passed by, as well as people on the sidewalk, waving.

"There's my mother!" cried Olivia Davidson.

Winston's voice boomed out in the darkness. "There I am again!"

All around the room, people yelled out in excitement. The room was buzzing with enthusiasm. Everyone seemed to love the video. In the darkness Elizabeth felt Jeffrey slip his arm around her.

For the rest of the hour, the documentary was punctuated by riotous laughter and cries of admiration. Despite Jessica's two embarrassing scenes—with Winston and Prince Albert—she came across as a poised, attractive professional. And the hours of editing at the television station had paid off, too. As a pink-orange-and-gold sunset faded into darkness on the screen, the crowd in the Wakefield living room burst into wild applause.

Elizabeth had never felt so happy and satisfied in her life.

"OK, everyone," Jessica yelled above the clamor. "Time to party!"

As the music began, people paired off to dance or wandered into the dining room, where soft drinks and snacks had been set up on the table. Detaching herself from a group of friends who were congratulating her, Elizabeth made her way across the room to Enid, who was sitting in a chair in a corner, her knees pulled up to her chin.

Enid looked up. "Hi. It was really great, Liz."

"Why didn't you come up front with us to get your share of the congratulations?" Elizabeth asked, squatting down beside Enid. "I would have told everyone you helped, but you looked as though you didn't want to be noticed."

Enid swallowed hard and quickly nodded her head. "You're right," she said in a slightly choked tone.

For a moment Elizabeth was silent. "Come on," she said finally, holding out her hand and standing up.

"What?"

"We're going up to my room to talk," Elizabeth said firmly. She pulled Enid to her feet and marched her up the stairs.

"Now," she said, shutting her bedroom door and leaning against it. "Once and for all, Enid. Out with it. What happened tonight? Where's Hugh, and why do you look like you're about to collapse?"

Enid sat down on the bed. "I—I—" She broke off, and then the tears came in a rush.

Elizabeth hurried to her friend and put her arms around her, letting her cry. Enid sobbed as though she would never stop.

"Come on, Enid. Don't worry," Elizabeth whispered soothingly. She reached for the box of tissues by her bed and handed one to Enid. "Everything will be fine."

"You don't understand." Enid sniffled and wiped her nose. "I don't even understand it myself."

Elizabeth brushed the hair away from Enid's tear-streaked face. "Just tell me."

With many starts and stops and bouts of crying, the whole long story came out: how Enid's grandmother had been taking advantage of her; how she had manipulated Enid and Mrs. Rollins to set them against each other; and how she had destroyed Enid's relationship with Hugh.

"But the worst thing is what I said to her before I left," she said shakily. She wiped her eyes and looked at Elizabeth with such grief and regret that Elizabeth felt tears come to her own eyes.

"I told her I hated her," she confessed in a low voice. "I told her I wished she'd never moved in with us."

"Oh, Enid. No!"

Miserable, Enid nodded. "I never should have said it. I know how much it must have hurt—it hurt so much to say it! And ever since I got here, I've had the feeling that something awful is going to happen."

"Well, things will calm down. You can apologize later, and maybe it will be a chance to get everything out into the open—discuss things with her, tell her how you feel."

Enid shook her head emphatically. "No," she insisted, jumping suddenly to her feet. "Something awful is going to happen, I know it. I should go. I should go right now. She might be sick. I might have made her sick," she went on, staring wildly at Elizabeth. "I've got to go home and see if she's all right."

"Enid, wait!" Elizabeth cried. "You're not being reasonable."

Enid pulled the door open and raced downstairs. Elizabeth ran after her, but it was no use: Enid was out the front door before Elizabeth reached the downstairs hallway.

Fourteen

Enid turned off the ignition and stared at her house, fighting off panic. No lights were on. Swallowing hard, she jumped out and ran up to the door, her hands trembling.

"Nana?" she called out.

Enid's heart hammered wildly in her chest, and she dashed into the darkened living room. Empty. Then she took the stairs two at a time and swung open the door of her old bedroom. There was no one there, either.

"Oh, no," she breathed, trying to collect her thoughts. She checked the bathroom, and her mother's bedroom, and even went up to the attic. There was no sign of her grandmother.

What have I done? she cried to herself. She knew she was responsible for whatever had happened to her grandmother. As tears of fear and shame welled up in her eyes, Enid paused for a moment at the head of the stairs and drew a deep breath to steady herself.

Then her head jerked up. *What was that smell?* She sniffed again. *Ginger?*

As slowly as a sleepwalker, Enid went down the stairs and to the back of the house, to the kitchen. The spicy-sweet aroma grew stronger. She pushed open the swinging door from the dining room and stepped into a bright, glowing warmth.

Leaning over in front of the oven, Mrs. Langevin pulled out a baking sheet of gingersnaps and set them down to cool. At the sound of Enid's gasp of surprise, she straightened, wiping her hands on her apron.

Enid stared at her grandmother's rosy cheeks, sparkling eyes, and warm, loving smile. "Nana?" she whispered, dazed. "What—?"

With a faint smile, Mrs. Langevin nodded toward the table. "Sit down, Enid. I've got something to say."

Enid obeyed automatically, too confused and relieved and surprised to wonder what her grandmother was going to tell her. Mrs. Langevin pulled out a chair and sat across from her.

"Enid, I've been doing a lot of thinking since you left tonight. Probably more thinking than I've done in a long time. What you said to me—"

"Nana—"

"Let me finish," Mrs. Langevin pleaded, holding up one hand. "It was a shock, let me tell you. But it was a shock because it was true!" She shook her head, as though she couldn't believe what she had done. "Ever since your grandfather died, I've been feeling sorry for myself, feeling like an old, helpless woman. And that's what I became."

"When I got here—seeing you and your mother so involved in exciting things, your friends, your boyfriends, your interests and careers—" She broke off and smiled ruefully. "I guess I was afraid I wouldn't get enough attention. So I made sure that I would—the only way I thought I could. And I realized tonight what a mistake that was."

Enid felt her heart swell with relief and love. "Oh, Nana!" She pressed her lips together to keep them from trembling.

Mrs. Langevin held out her hand, and Enid grasped it quickly. "I was doing everything I could to keep you, and I ended up making you hate me."

"Nana, I didn't mean it! I'm so sorry I said it," Enid said, gripping her grandmother's hand.

"No—it's all right, dear. I hated that person, too, when I took a good look at her—nagging, complaining, whining." She chuckled softly. "I'm so glad you showed me what I was doing before I lost you forever. I—I haven't lost you, have I?" she asked tremulously.

Enid jumped up from the table and enveloped her grandmother in a desperate hug. Tears of love and relief and happiness ran down both their faces. "I love you, Nana," Enid choked out. "I love you!"

For a long time, they hugged each other, crying and apologizing and sharing their feelings. After a while, Enid sat down in the chair next to her grandmother's and wiped her tears away.

"So, where do we go from here?" she asked with a tearful smile.

Mrs. Langevin pursed her lips and nodded thoughtfully. "Well, dear, I, for one, am going back to Chicago."

"No! Nana, why? I want you to stay with us!"

Enid's grandmother patted her hand. "I know, Enid. But I realize now that I have to come to terms with my old life. I'm just running away from it now." Another tear rolled down her cheek, and Enid realized with a pang that her grandmother was thinking about her dead husband. "But—I know I can do it. I'll stay with friends, at first, and look around for a small apartment in my old neighborhood. When I can truly say goodbye to my memories, maybe I'll come back and start making some new memories."

Enid didn't want her grandmother to leave now, but she thought she was beginning to understand. She nodded regretfully.

"There, dear. This is the best way. And I feel better tonight than I have in ages."

"Really, Nana?"

Mrs. Langevin regarded Enid tenderly. "Yes, Enid. Thank you."

A sob threatened to rise to the surface again, and Enid stifled it with a laugh. "Oh—anytime."

Just then the door bell rang.

"Who could that be?" Enid wondered aloud. She pushed herself up from the table and hurried to the front.

Enid's heart skipped a beat when she saw who was standing on the doorstep. "Hugh?" she said in surprise.

A pink blush spread over his face. "I had to tell you I'm sorry, Enid. I acted like a jerk tonight."

At first, Enid was too surprised to respond. But in one sense, she wasn't surprised at all. Already she had made up with her grandmother more happily than she could have hoped. She felt a huge smile spreading across her face.

"I wouldn't blame you if you don't want to keep going out with me," Hugh muttered, still looking down and oblivious to her jubilant expression. "But I just wanted to apologize. You're a really special person, and I admire you for the way you've been sticking up for your grandmother." He gulped. "So . . . goodbye." He turned to walk back down the steps.

"Hugh, you idiot. Come back here."

Wide-eyed, he turned around, and Enid threw herself into his arms.

"How could I resist an apology like that?" She laughed and then stood back to look into his eyes. She laughed again at the relief and happiness she saw there and tugged at his hand. "Come on inside and meet my grandmother."

He swallowed, then exhaled slowly. "Sure," he said with a happy smile. "OK."

The three of them were gorging themselves on gingersnaps and milk and playing a wild game of charades when Mrs. Rollins walked into the kitchen at eleven o'clock.

"What on earth—?"

Enid whirled around and let out a whoop. "Mom! How was the awards dinner? Did Richard win anything?"

"No . . ." Dazed, Mrs. Rollins put her evening bag down on the table and stared at the plate of cookies. She looked at Hugh. She looked at her mother's beaming face.

"Well, he should have," Enid continued breathlessly, helping her mother out of her coat.

"Thank you, Enid. Hello, Hugh. Mother?"

"Adele, I swear you look awfully peaked," Mrs. Langevin said airily as she rose to get another carton of milk from the refrigerator. "You look like you could use some of my special-recipe gingersnaps."

Mrs. Rollins looked at each of them again and folded her arms across her chest. "All right. What on earth is going on here?"

"Enid and I had a talk," her mother explained with a smile as she poured some milk. "I'm going back to Chicago for a while to straighten some things out." She and Enid exchanged a meaningful look.

As she sank slowly into a chair, Mrs. Rollins gave them a puzzled frown. "I get the feeling there's a lot more to this," she said carefully. She frowned again and then broke into a wide, beautiful smile. "But for the time being, just pass me those cookies before they're all gone!"

"Whew!" Jessica let out a dramatic sigh as she threw herself back onto the couch and propped her legs up on the coffee table. "That was one great party, if I do say so myself. I can't believe how many people showed up."

The only guests left at the Wakefields' were Lila and Cara. Jessica closed her eyes blissfully and sank down deeper into the cushions. Then she opened one eye and glanced at Cara. Her friend still seemed moody and preoccupied, which puzzled Jessica. All evening she had kept a watch on Cara and her brother. On the surface things seemed to be fine. But she knew Cara, and she knew Steven. Things were not fine.

Lila yawned. "Speaking of people, Jess, did you invite Abbie? I was kind of surprised to see her here."

"No, I didn't. I guess Liz did—or she came with someone, I guess." Frowning, Jessica hugged a pillow to her. Seeing Abbie Richardson, a pretty brunette, at the party had been a surprise to her, too. In ninth grade, she and Lila had been friends with her. But Abbie had started going out with a boy from Palisades High sophomore year, and made it clear she wasn't interested in Lila or Jessica anymore.

"No," she repeated slowly. "I didn't know she was coming."

Lila shrugged and scraped together some potato chip crumbs from the bottom of the bowl. "I just wondered," she mumbled. From the corner of her eye, she shot a look at Cara and added, "I saw her dancing with Steven, and I didn't know they knew each other."

Jessica glanced at Cara again and was worried when she saw Cara's face flush slightly. Something was definitely up with Cara and Steven. And she was going to find out what it was.

Is trouble brewing between Cara and Steven? Find out in PRETENSES, *Sweet Valley High #44.*

MURDER AND MYSTERY STRIKES

SWEET VALLEY HIGH®

America's favorite teen series
has a hot new line
of
Super Thrillers!

It's super excitement, super suspense, and super thrills as Jessica and Elizabeth Wakefield put on their detective caps in the new SWEET VALLEY HIGH SUPER THRILLERS! Follow these two sleuths as they witness a murder . . . find themselves running from the mob . . . and uncover the dark secrets of a mysterious woman. SWEET VALLEY HIGH SUPER THRILLERS are guaranteed to keep you on the edge of your seat!

YOU'LL WANT TO READ THEM ALL!

☐ #1: DOUBLE JEOPARDY   26905-4/$2.95
☐ #2: ON THE RUN   27230-6/$2.95
☐ #3: NO PLACE TO HIDE   27554-2/$2.95
☐ #4: DEADLY SUMMER   28010-4/$2.95

- -

Bantam Books, Dept. SVH5, 414 East Golf Road, Des Plaines, IL 60016

Please send me the books I have checked above. I am enclosing $_____ (please add $2.00 to cover postage and handling). Send check or money order—no cash or C.O.D.s please.

Mr/Ms _____

Address _____

City/State _____ Zip _____

SVH5—7/89

Please allow four to six weeks for delivery. This offer expires 1/90.